TREAT

Word and pictures by Mary Sullivan

HOUGHTON MIFFLIN HARCOURT
Boston   New York

To my editor, Kate, for being my fan.
And to Carlos, Gemma, and Nico—for being my sunshine. —MS

All rights reserved. For information about permission to reproduce selections from
this book, write to Permissions, Houghton Mifflin Harcourt Publishing Company,
215 Park Avenue South, New York, New York 10003.

www.hmhco.com

The text of this book is set in Myriad Std Tilt.
The illustrations are pencil on Strathmore drawing paper, scanned and digitally colored.

ISBN 978-0-544-47270-9

Manufactured in Malaysia
TWP 10 9 8 7 6 5 4 3 2 1
4500560536

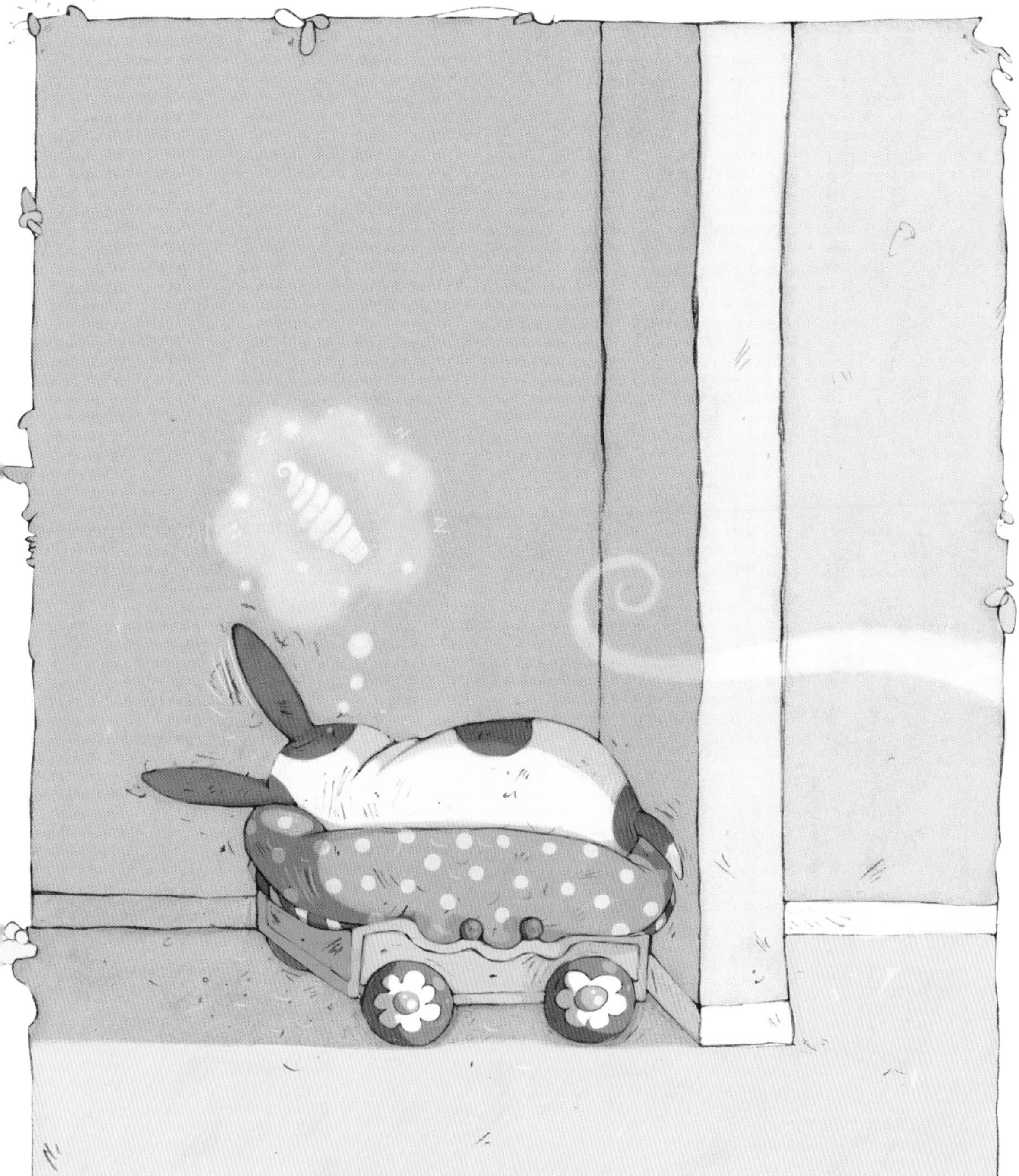

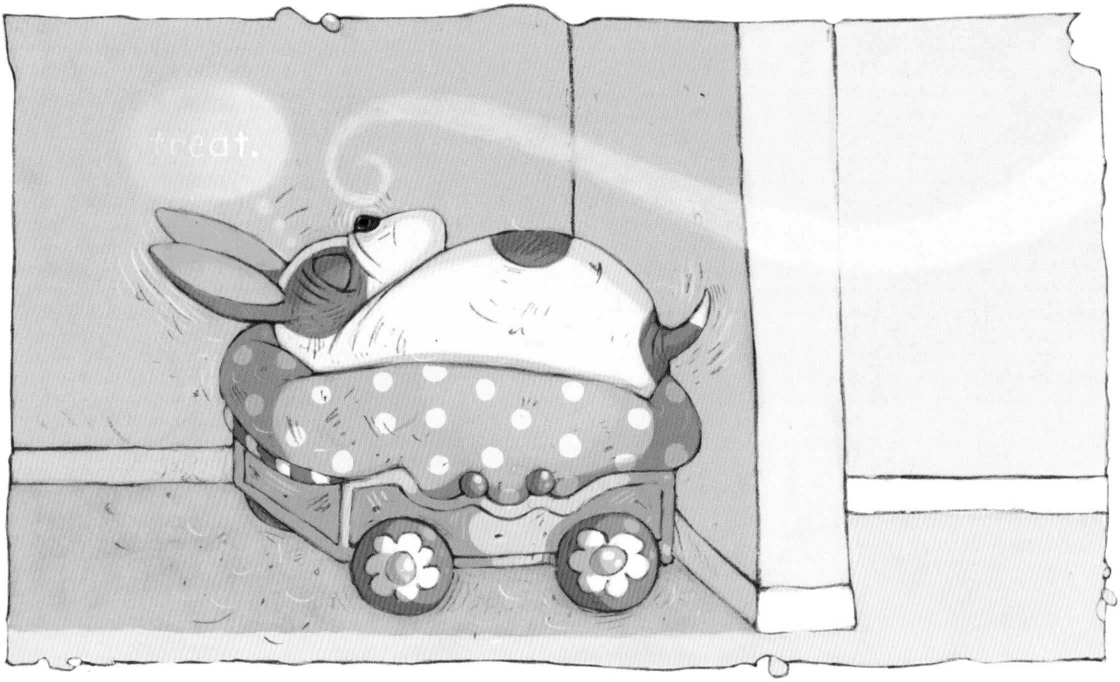
treat.

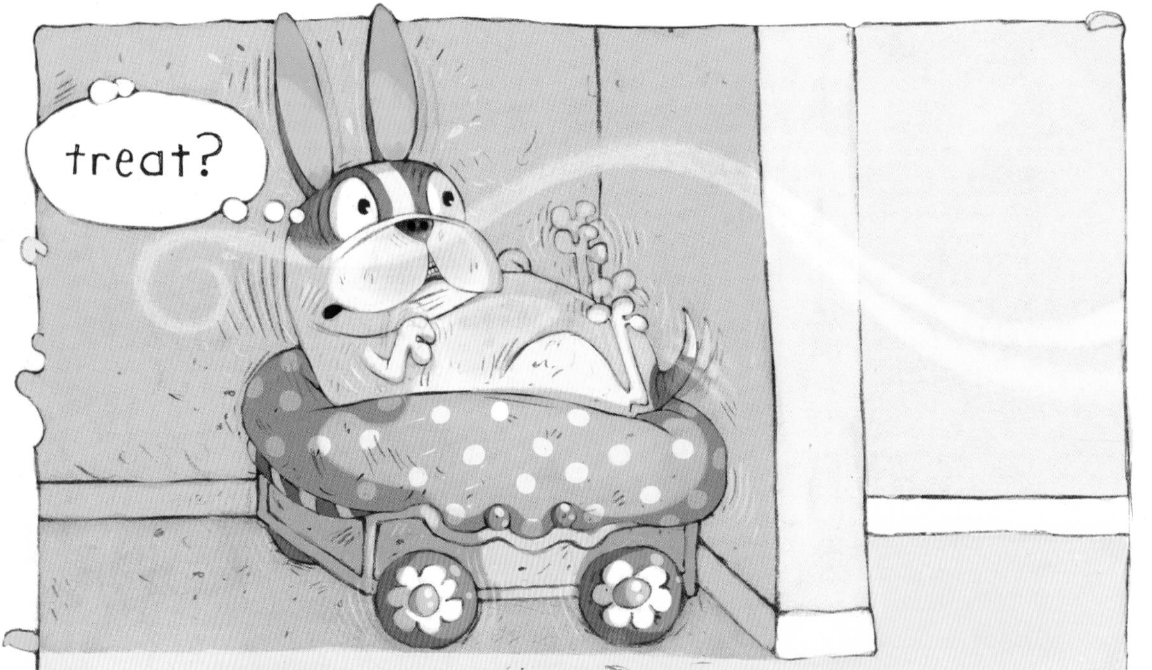
treat?

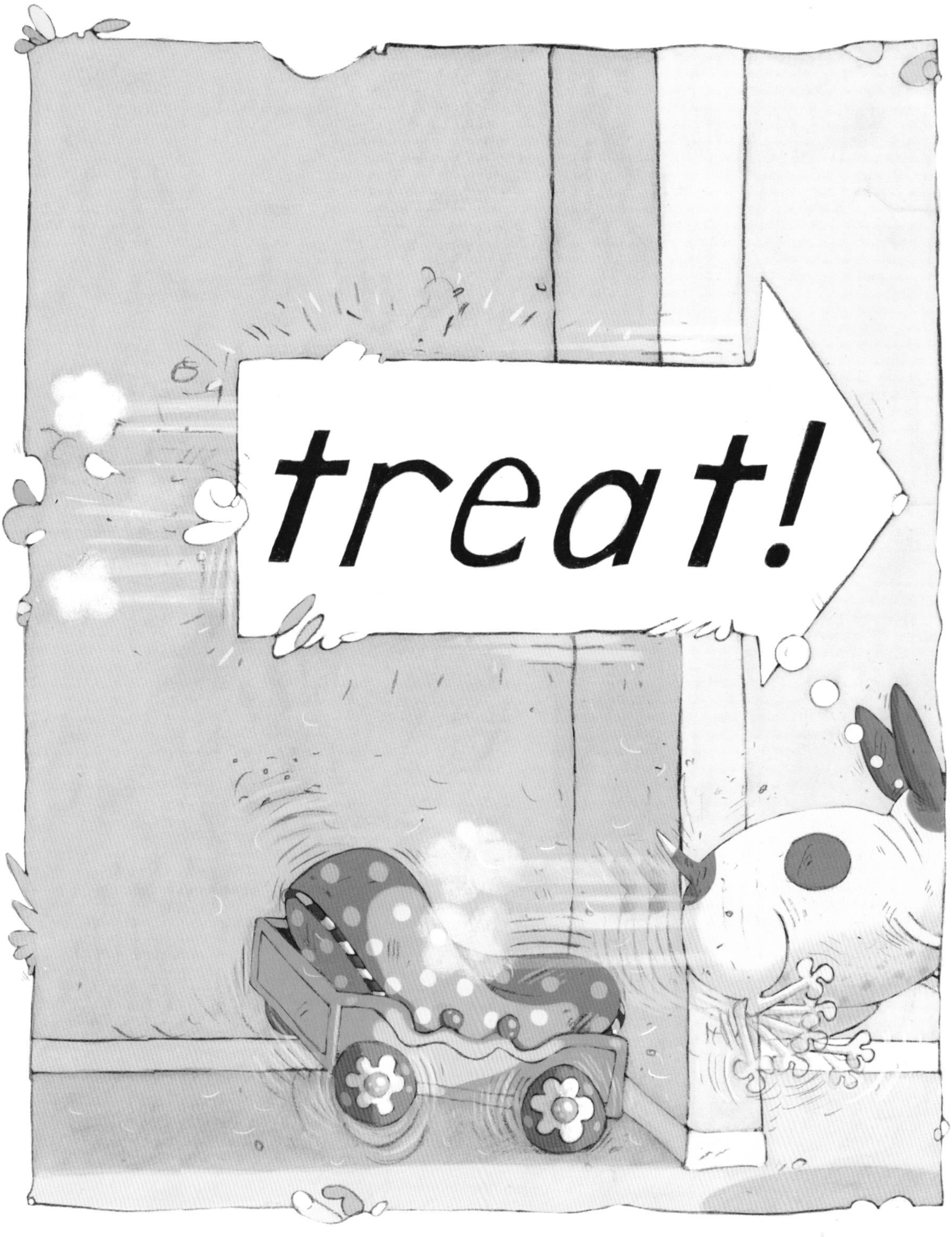
treat!

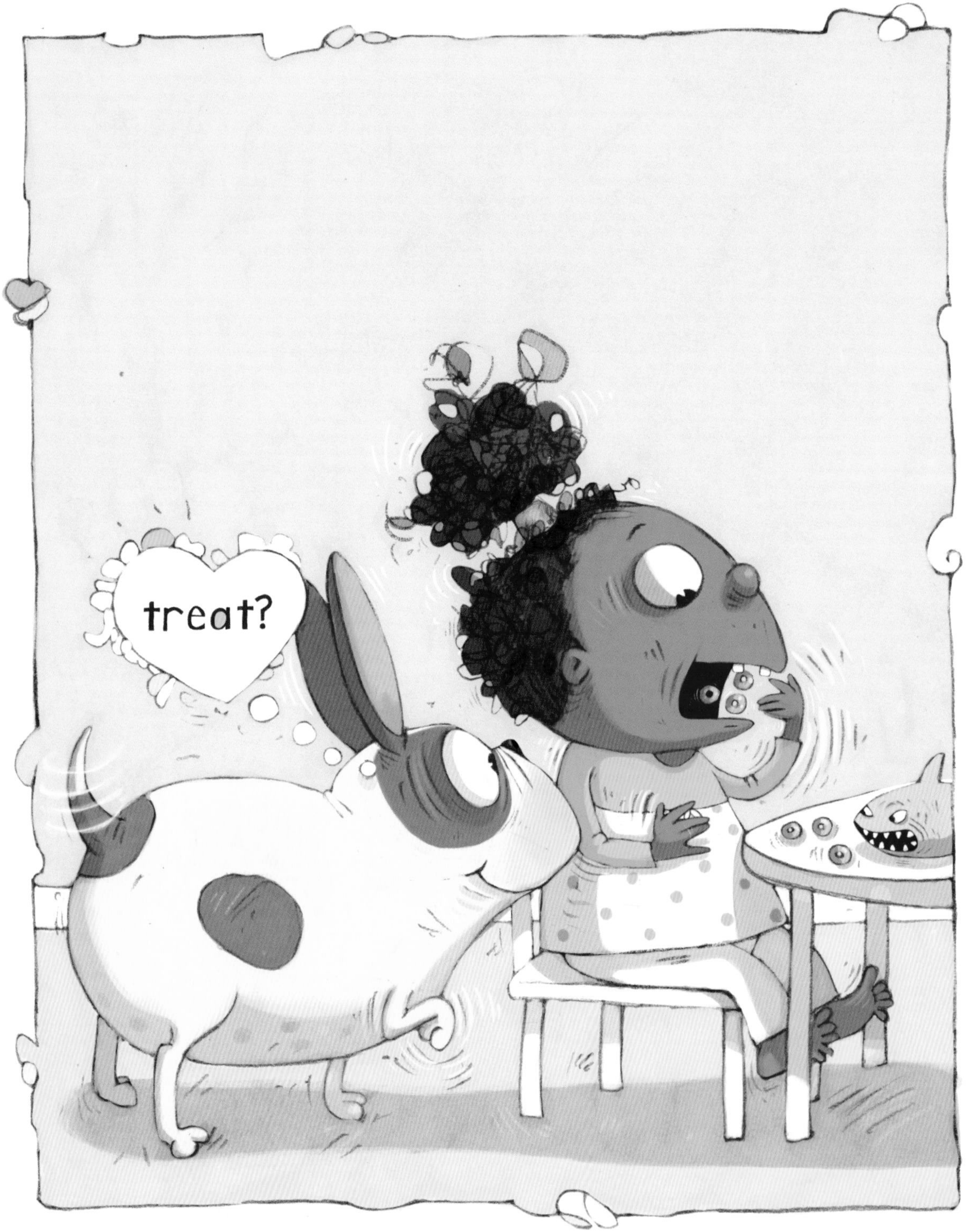
treat?

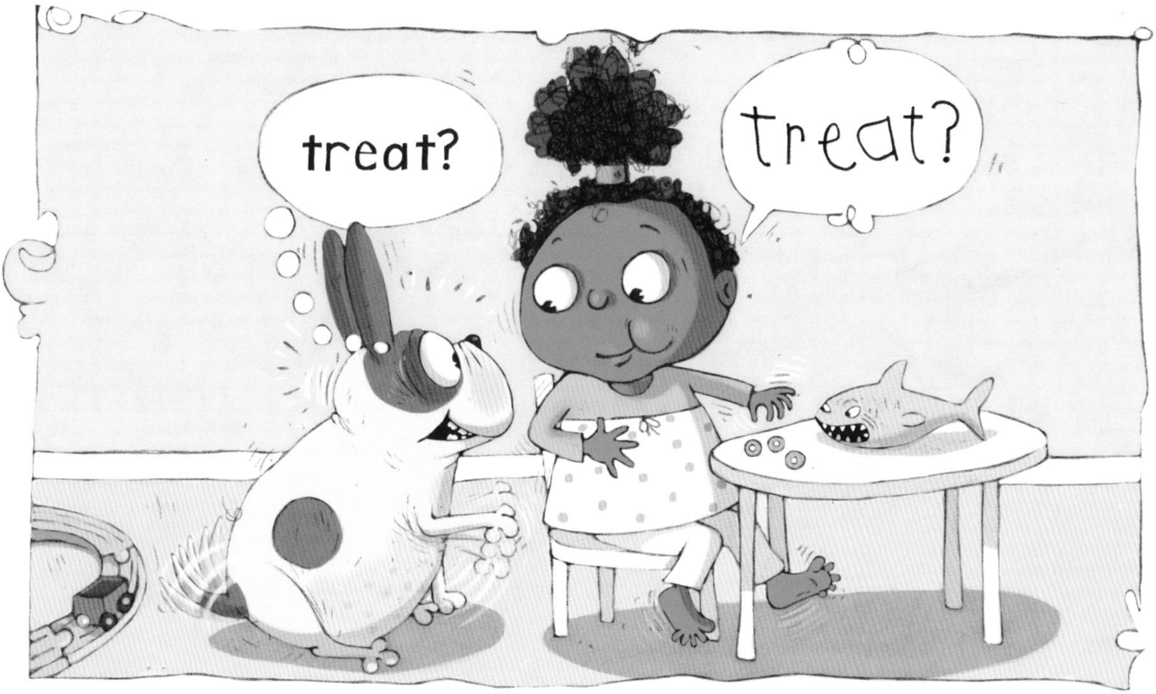
treat?
treat?

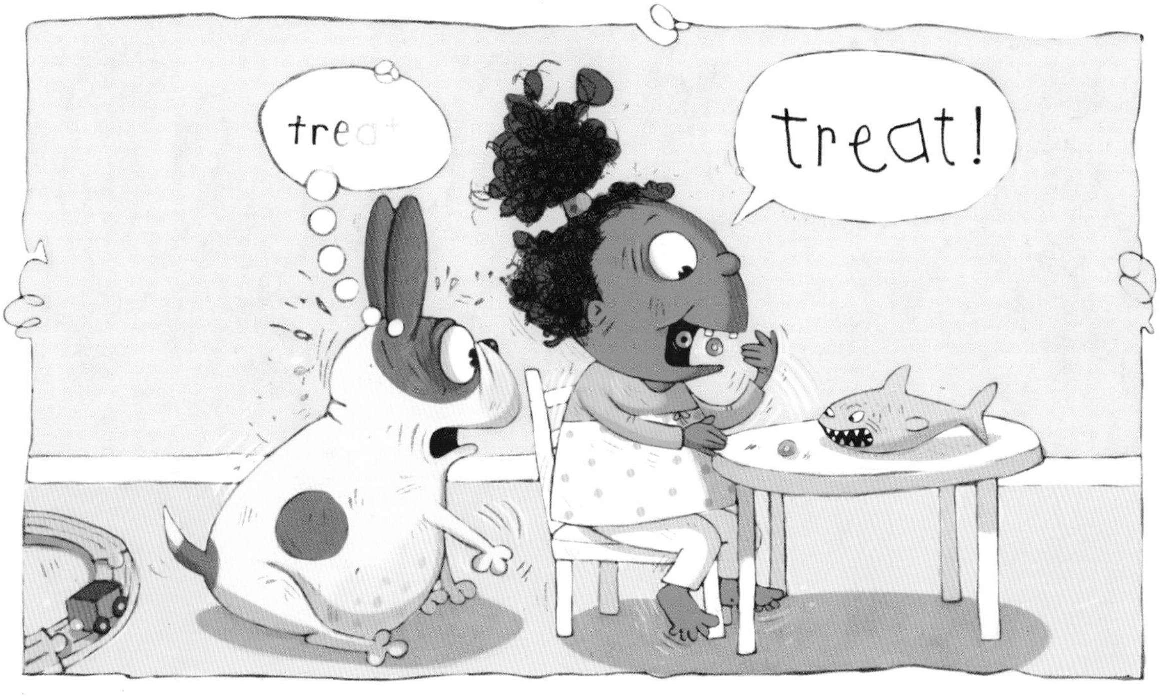
tre
treat!

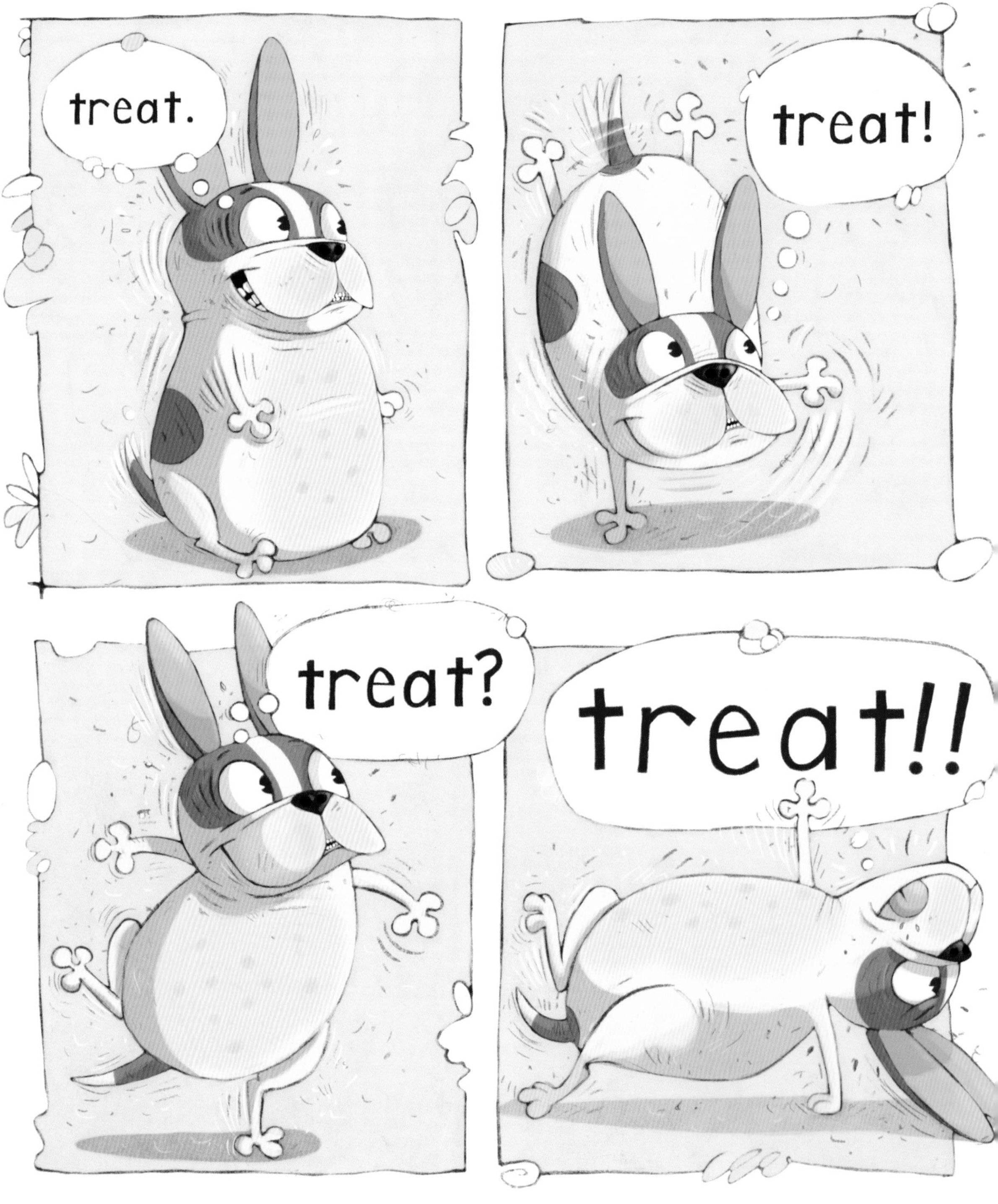
treat.
treat!
treat?
treat!!

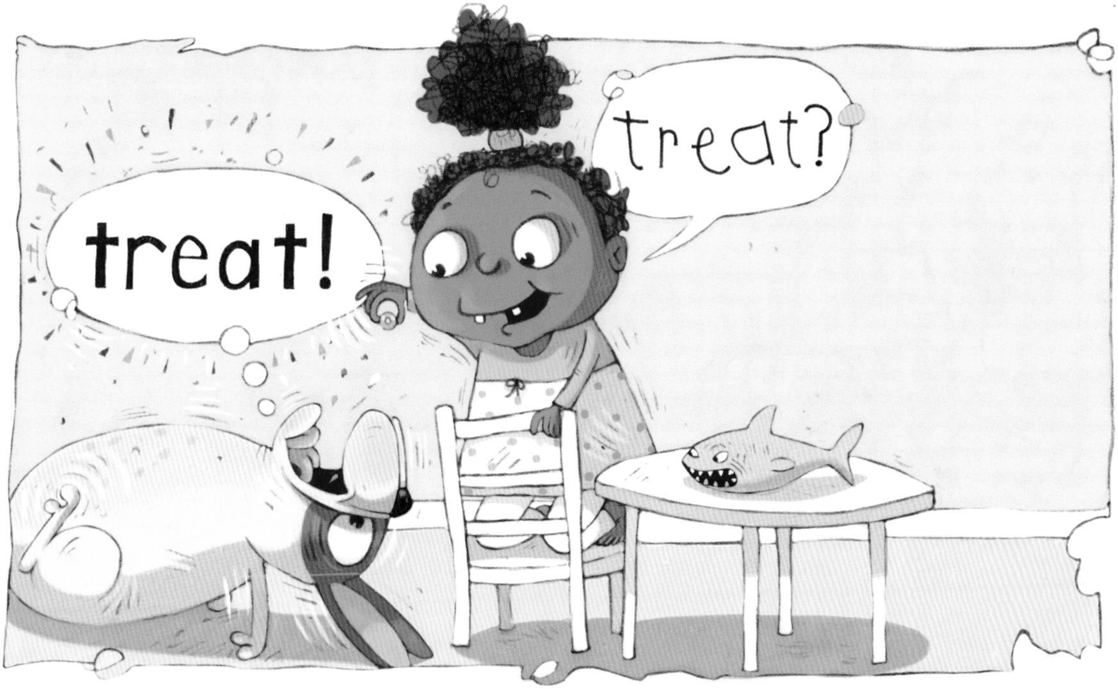
treat!
treat?

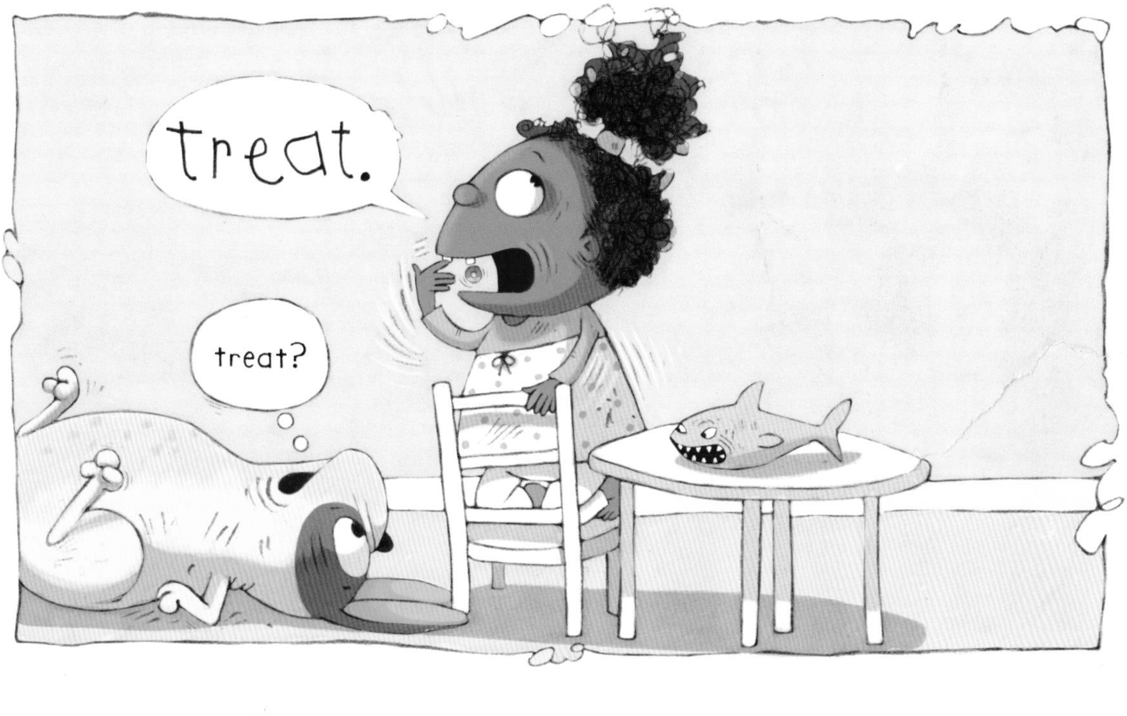
treat.
treat?

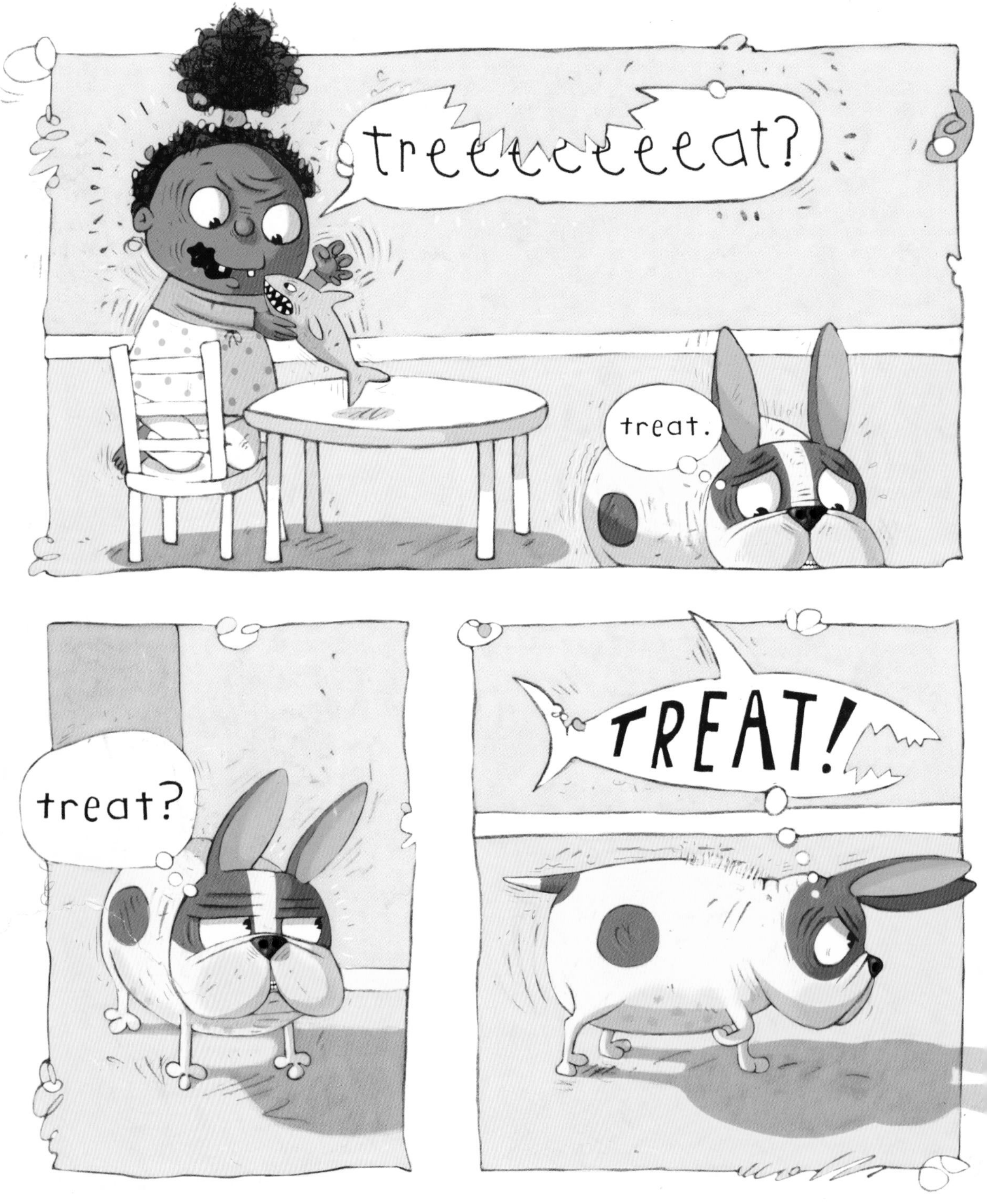
treeeeeeeat?
treat.
treat?
TREAT!

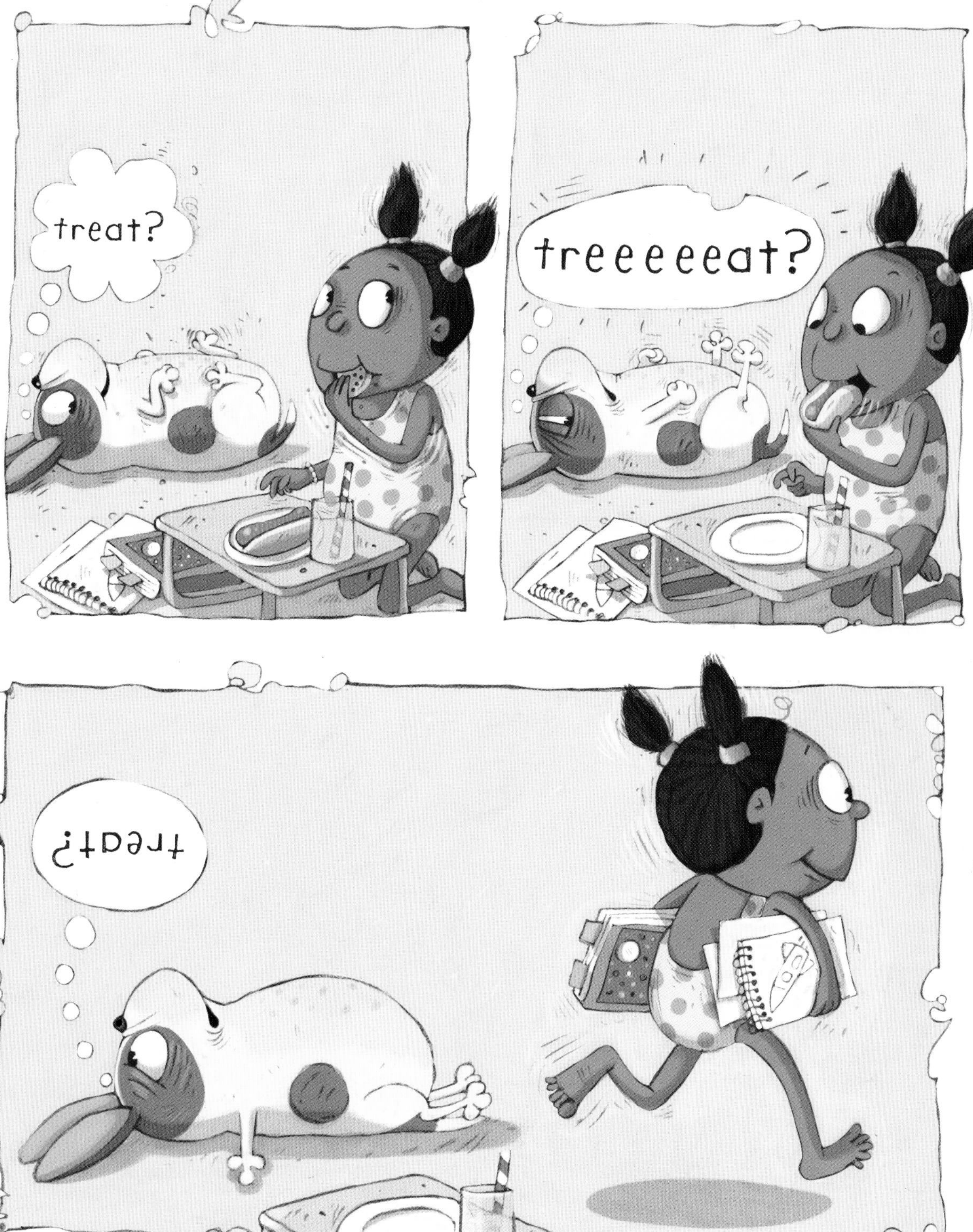
treat?
treeeeeat?
treat?

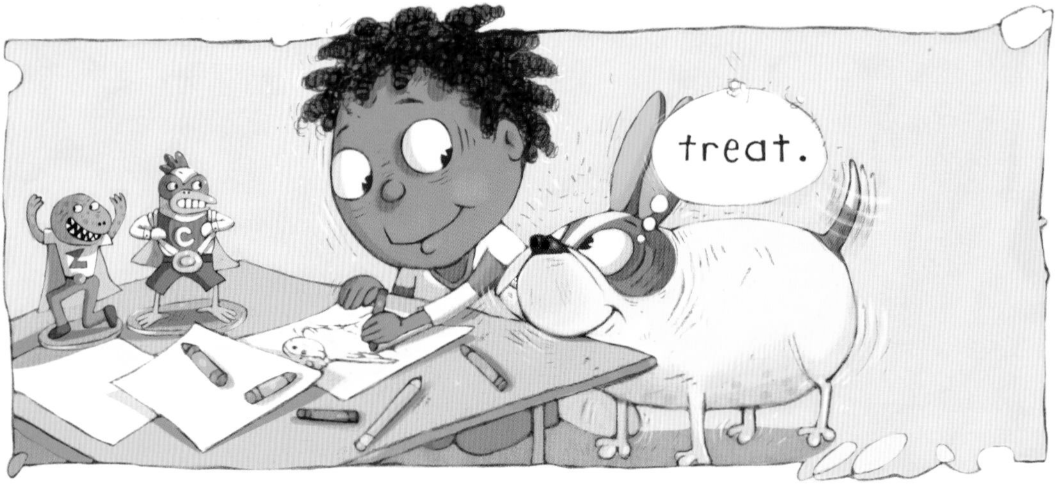
treat.

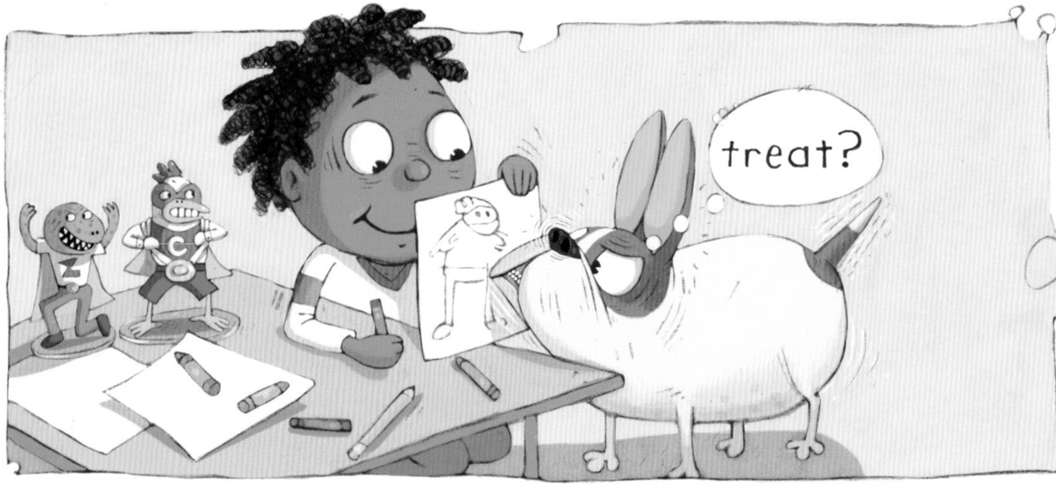
treat?

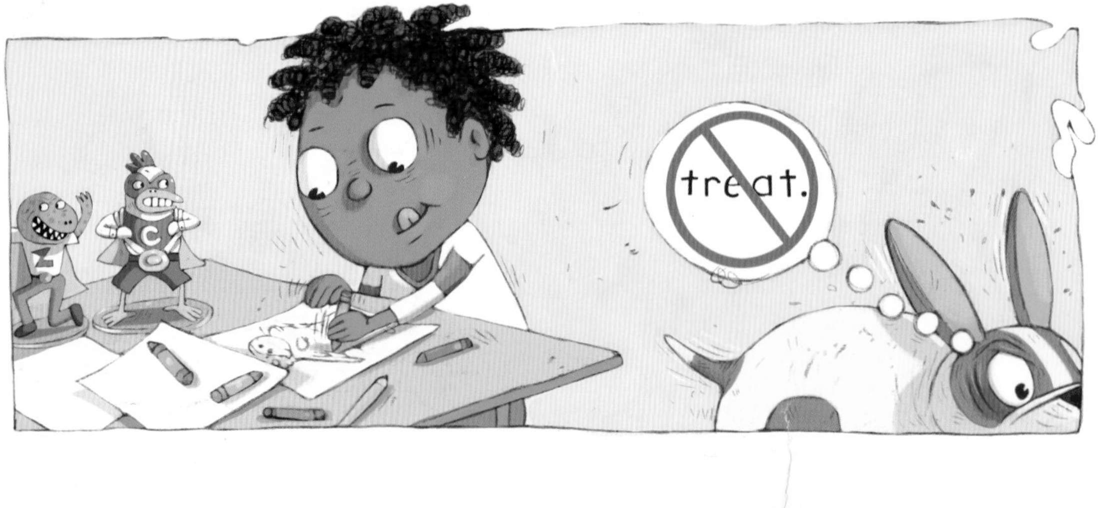
treat.

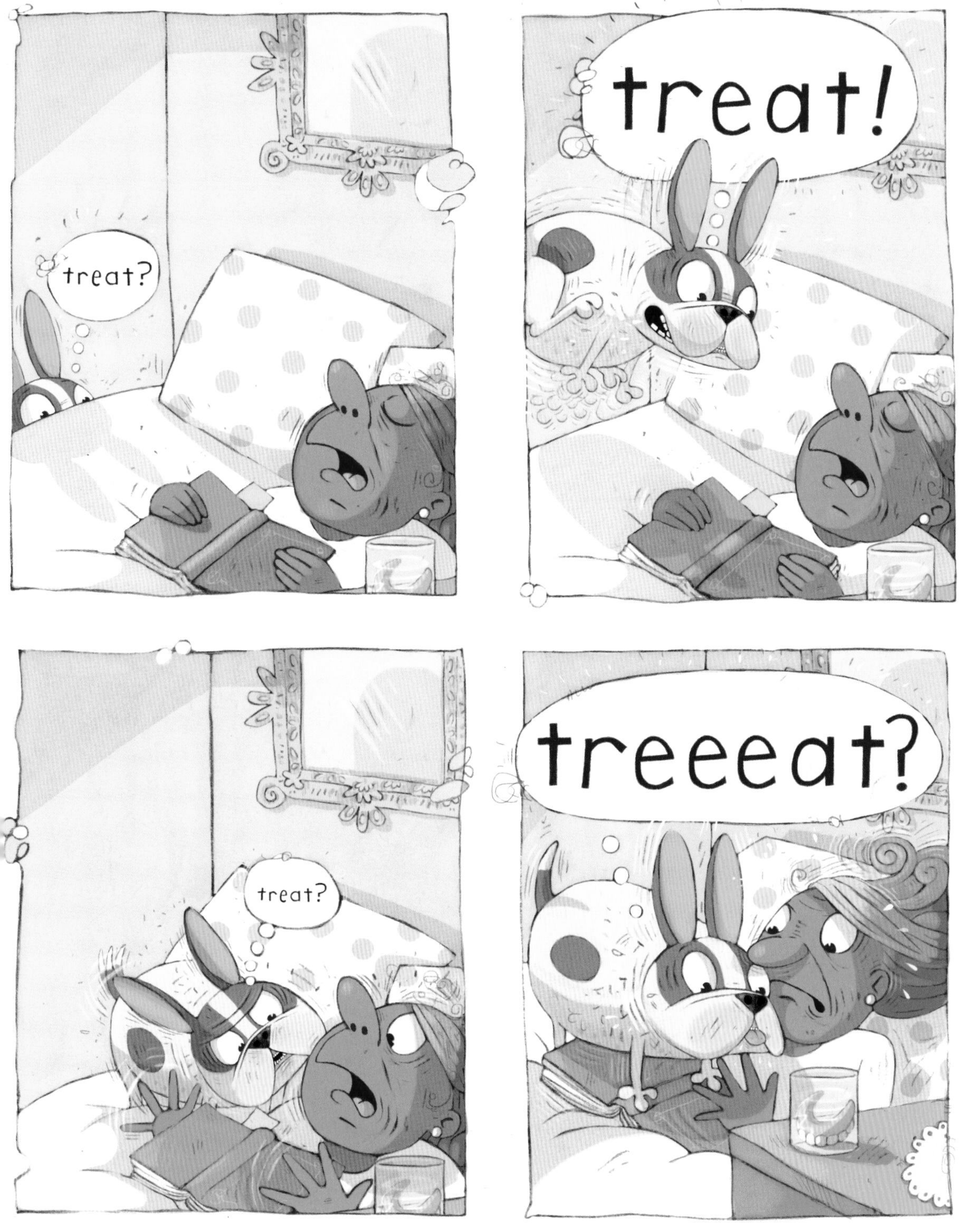
treat?
treat!
treat?
treeeat?

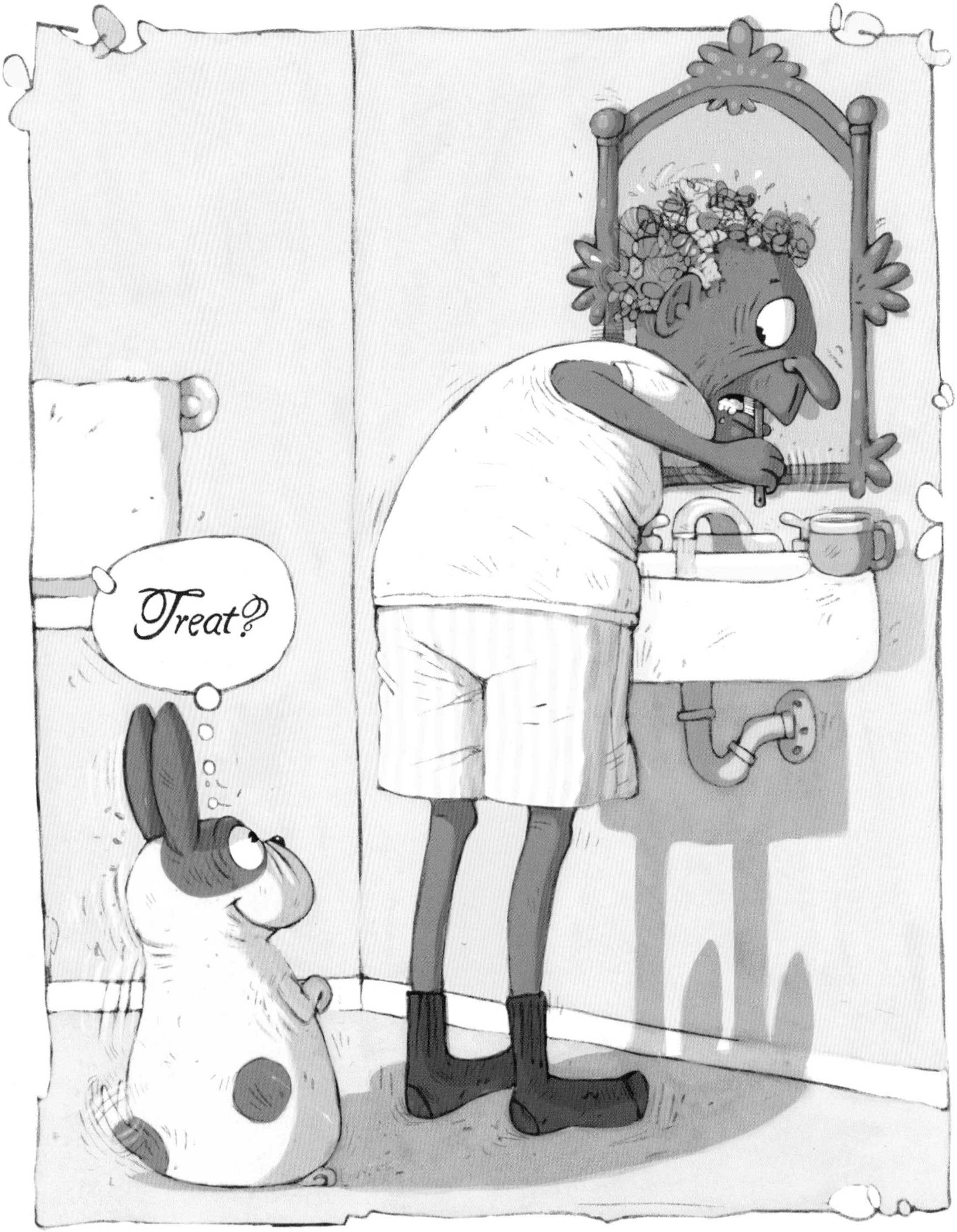
Treat?

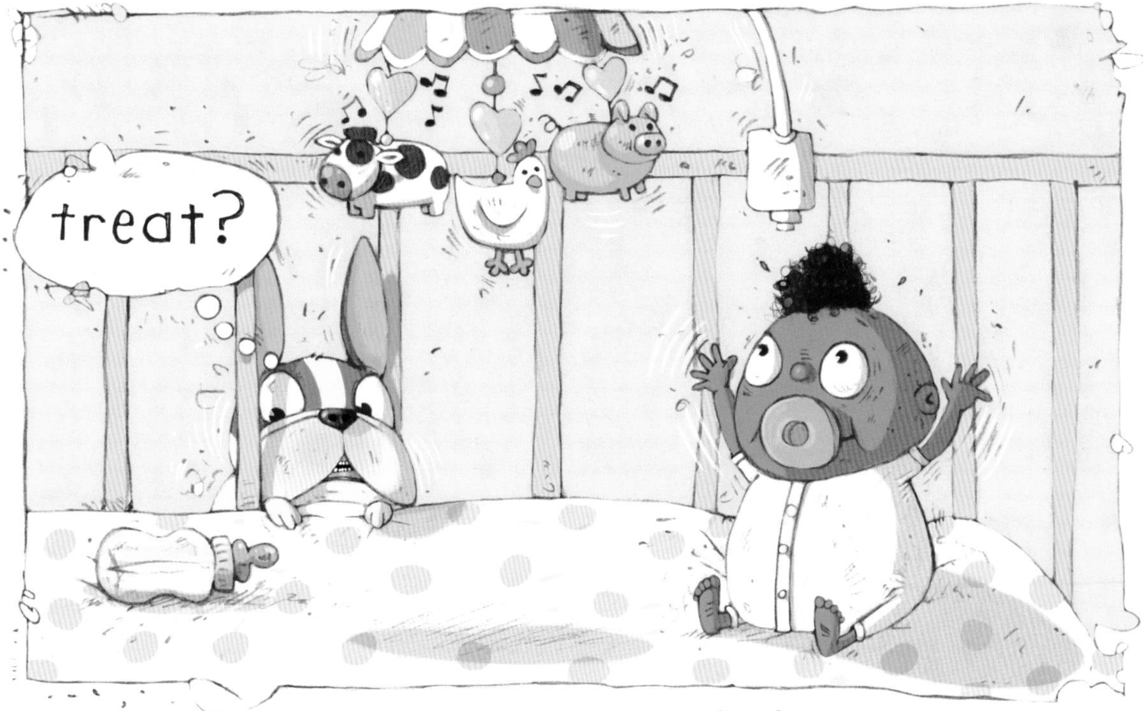
treat?

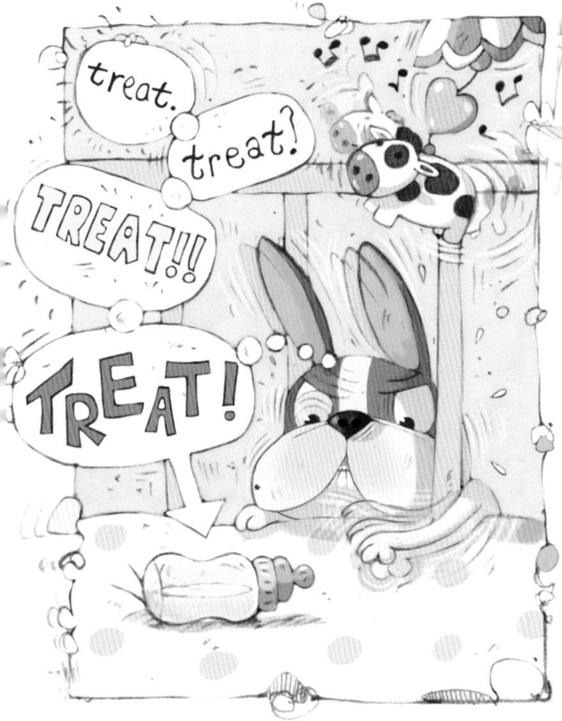
treat.
treat?
TREAT!!
TREAT!

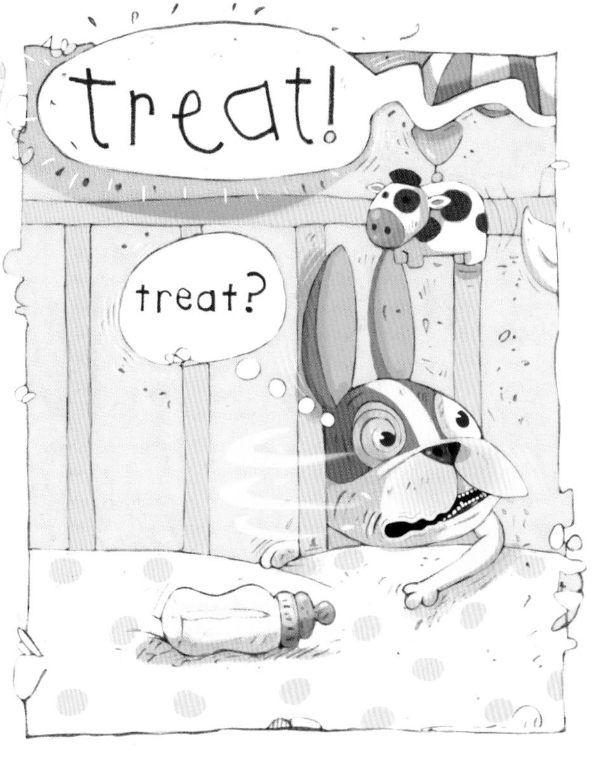
treat!
treat?

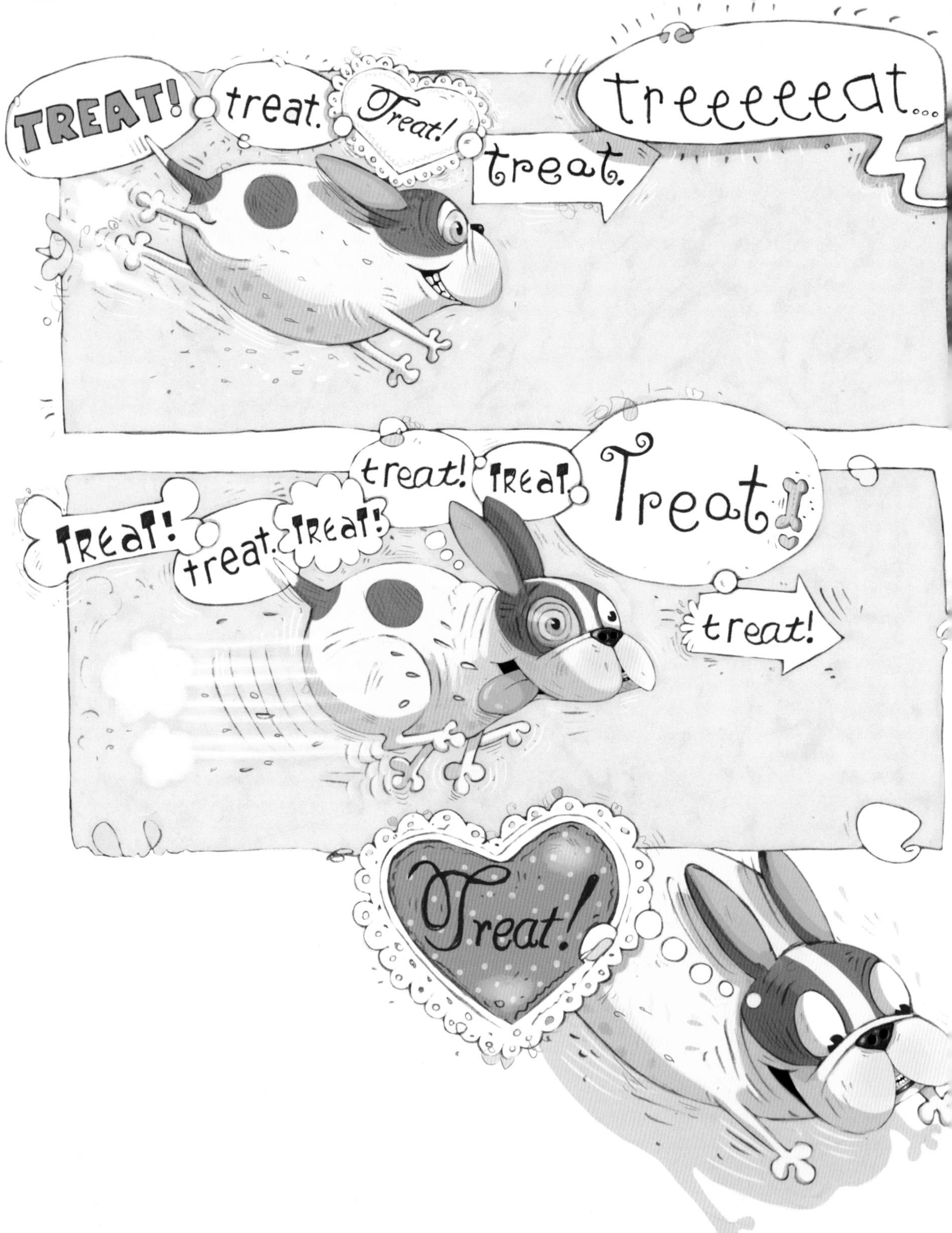
TREAT!
treat.
Treat!
treeeeeat...
treat.
TREAT!
treat.
TREAT!
treat!
TREAT.
Treat!
treat!
Treat!

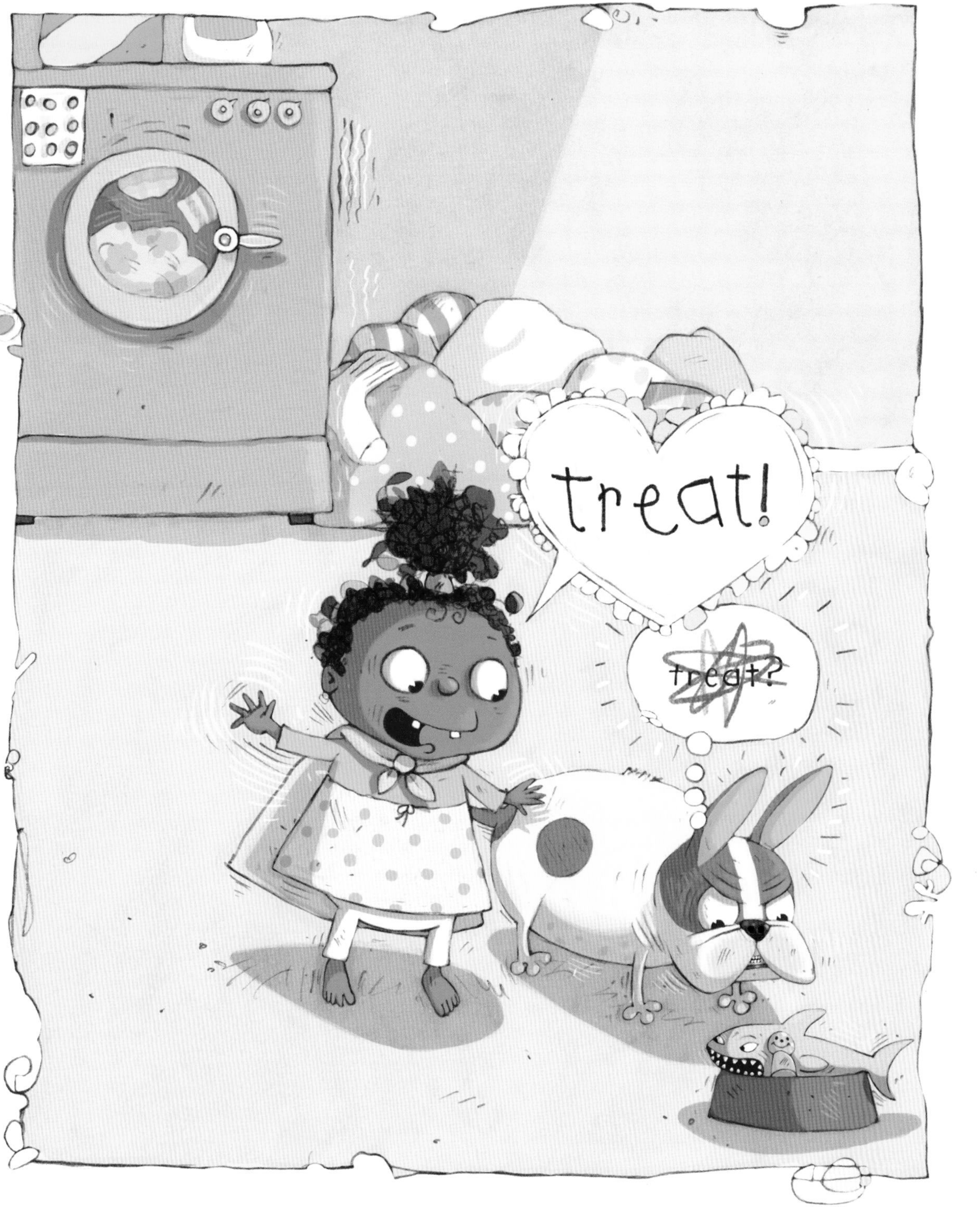
treat!
treat?

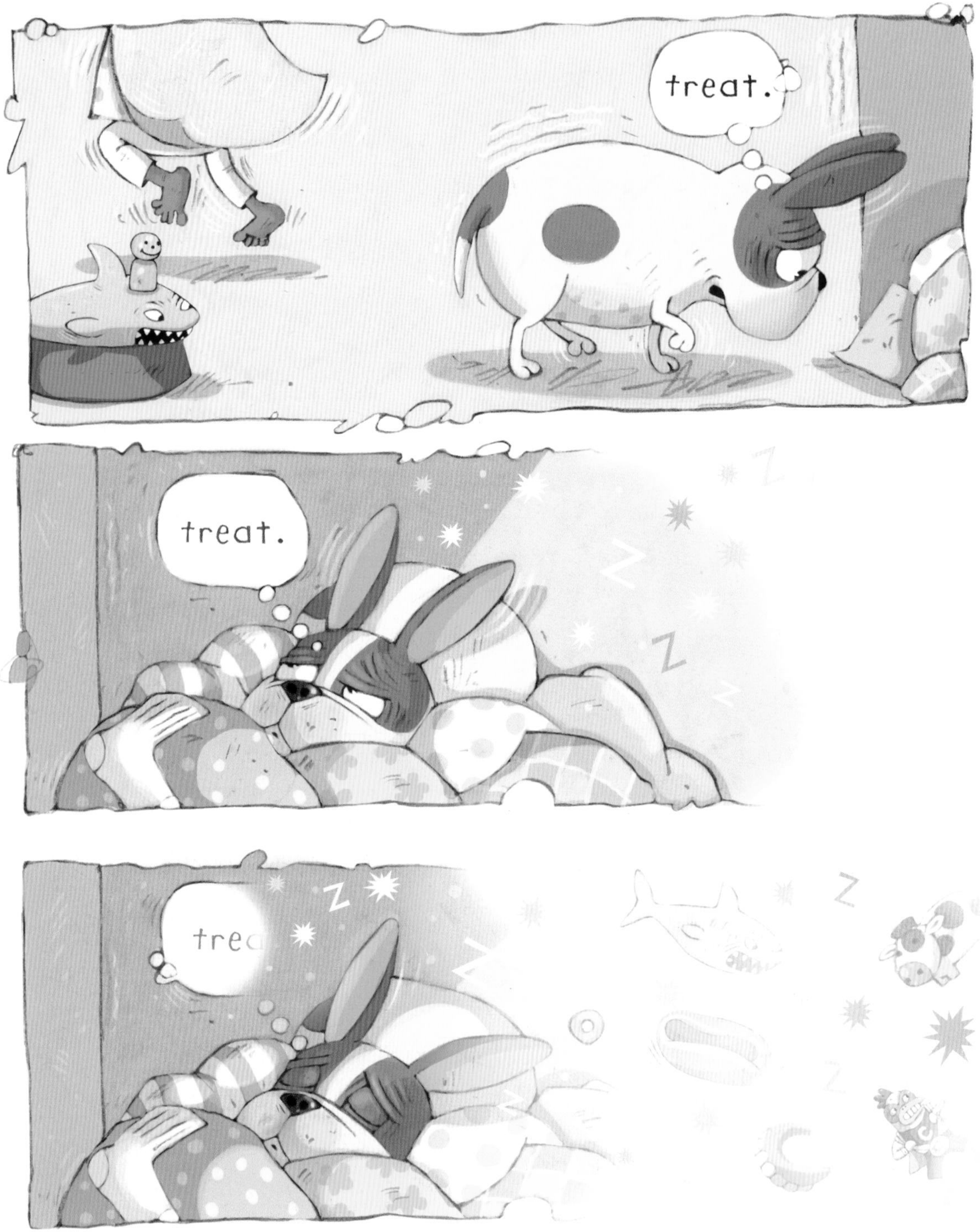
treat.
treat.
trea

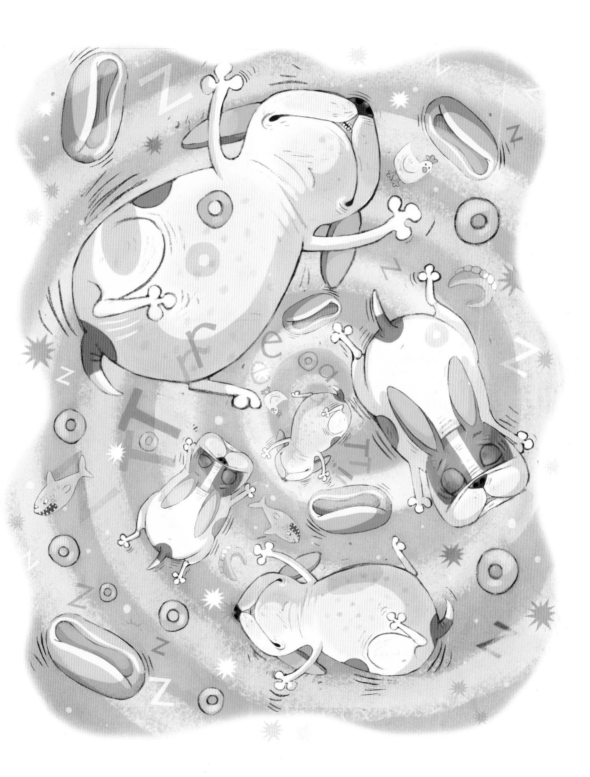

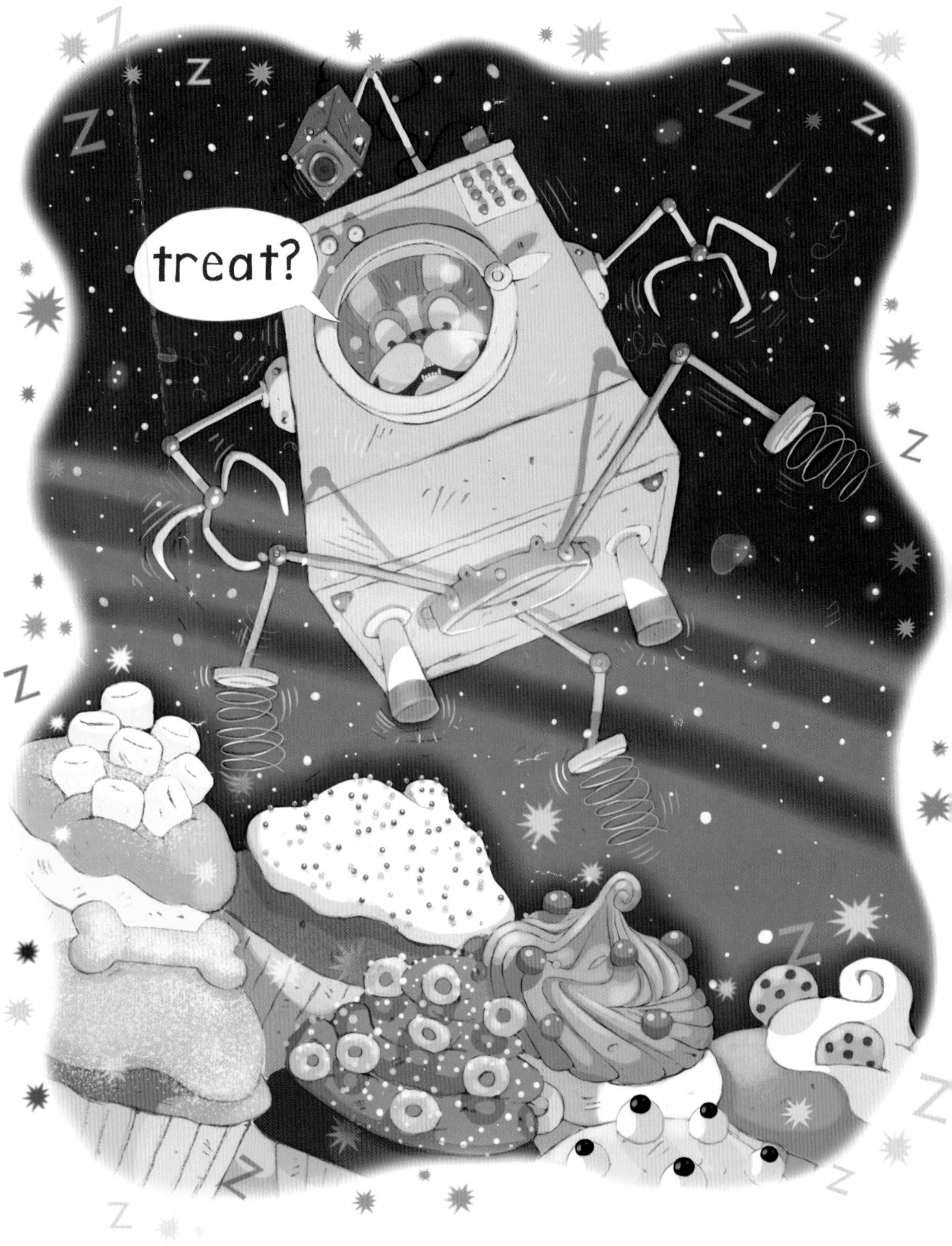
treat?

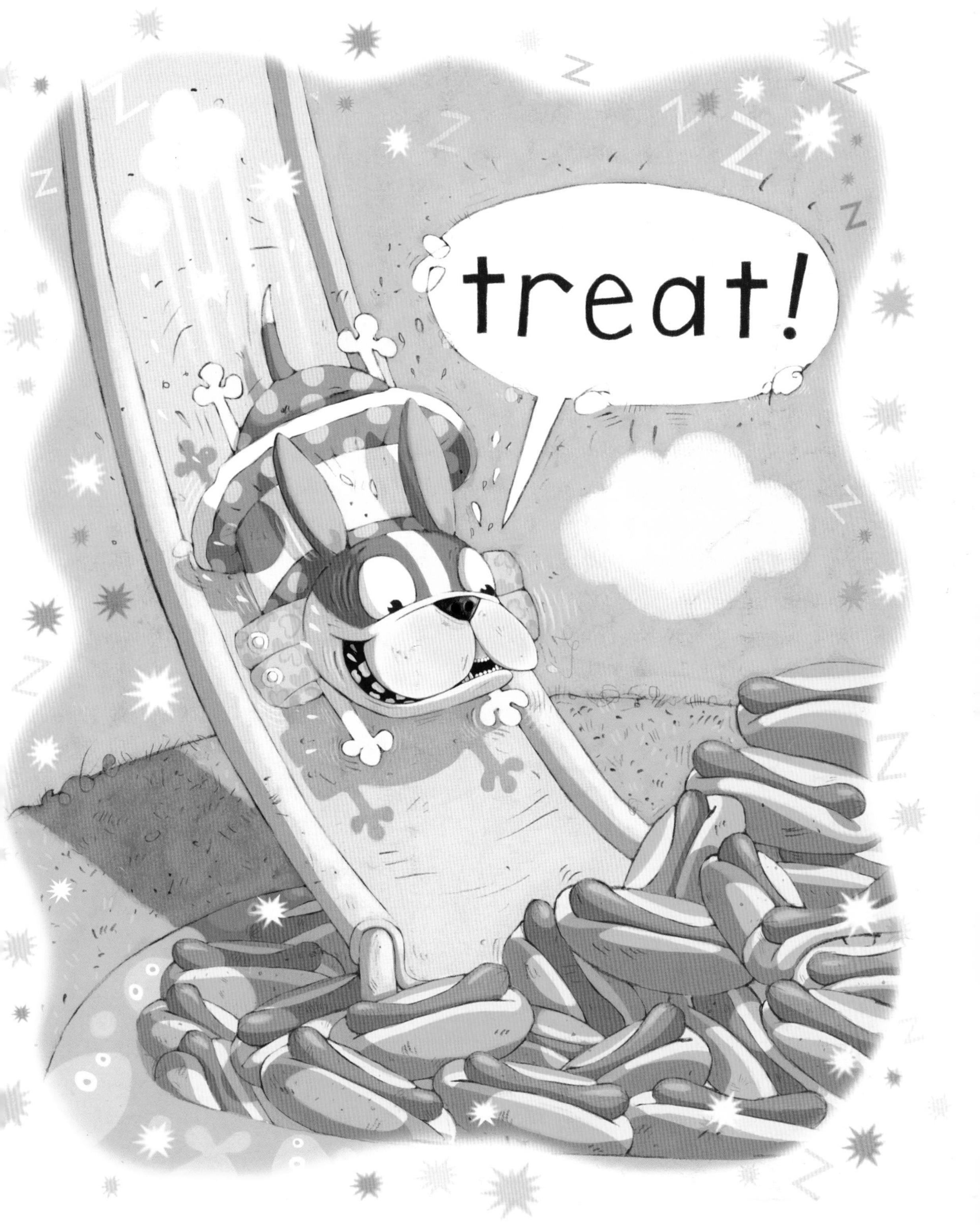
treat!

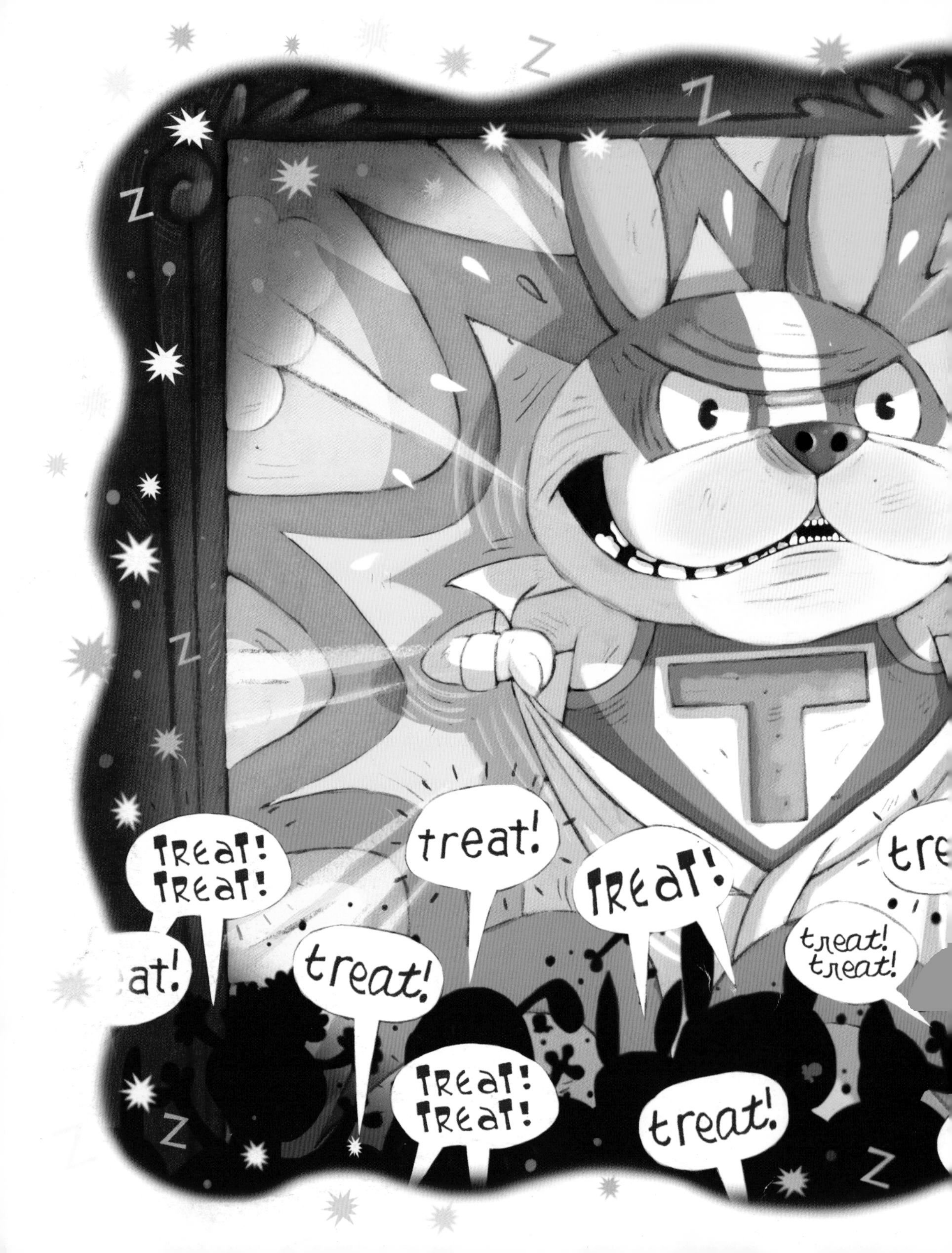
TREAT! TREAT!
treat!
TREAT!
tre
at!
treat!
treat! treat!
TREAT! TREAT!
treat!

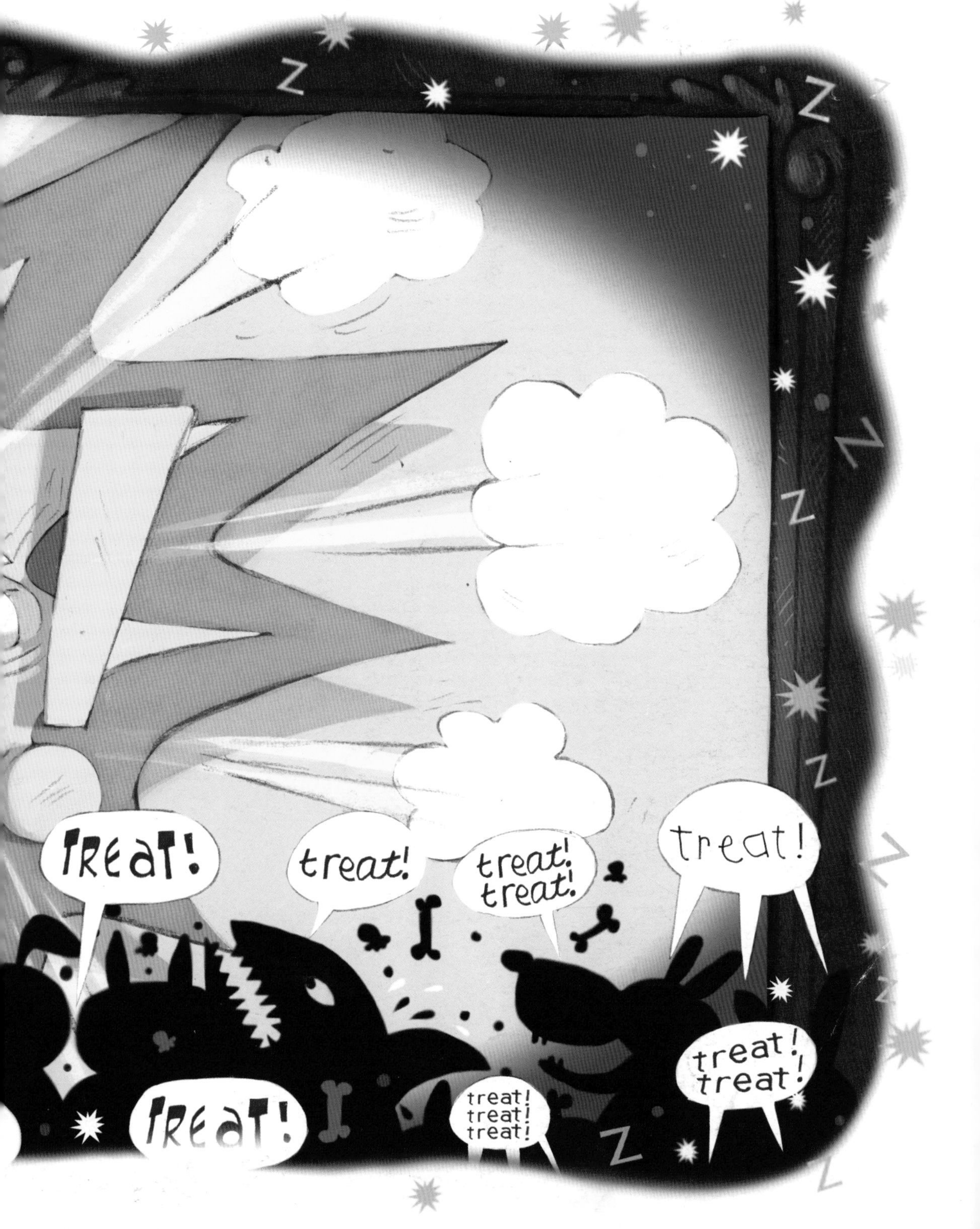
TREAT!
treat!
treat! treat!
treat!
TREAT!
treat! treat! treat!
treat! treat!

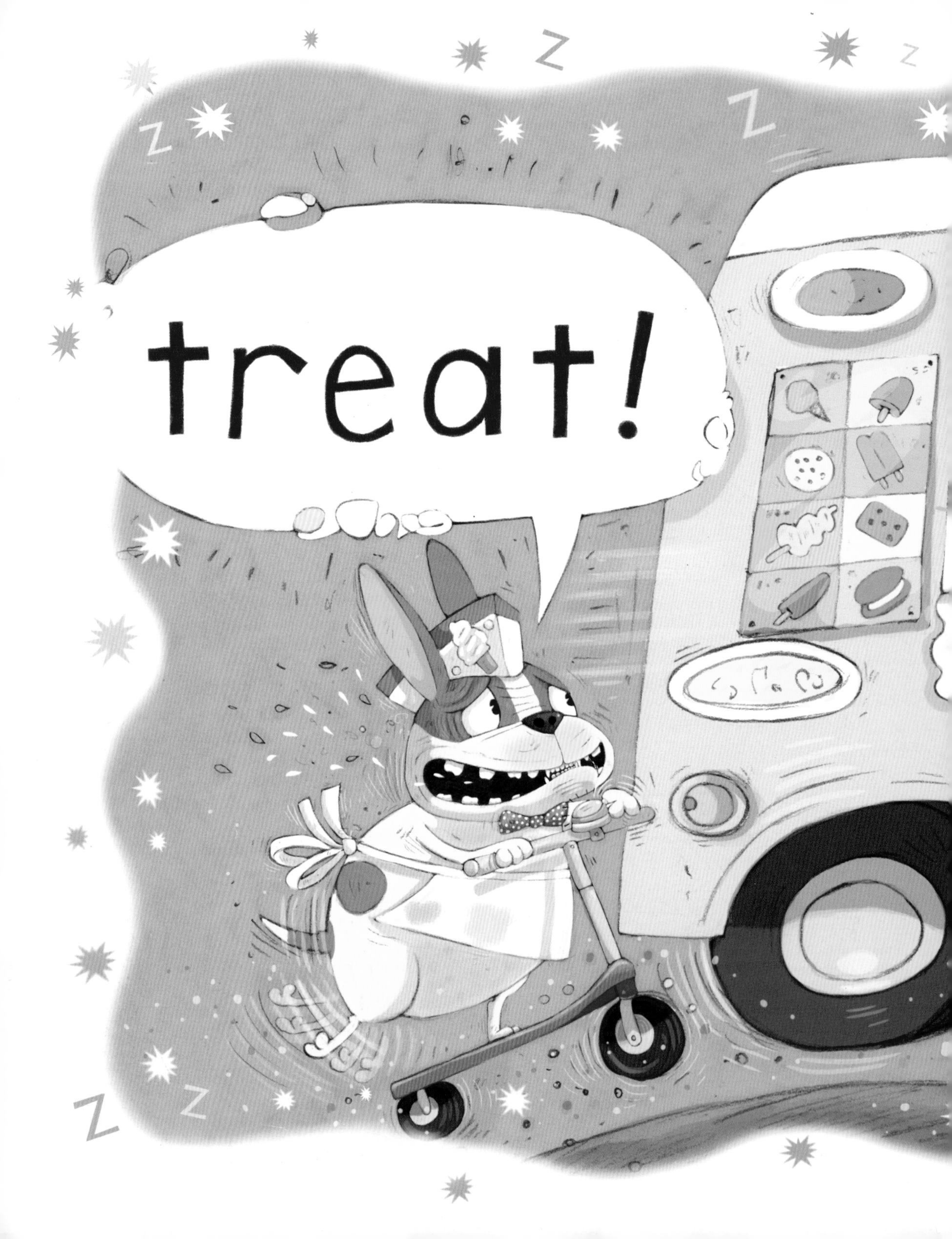
treat!

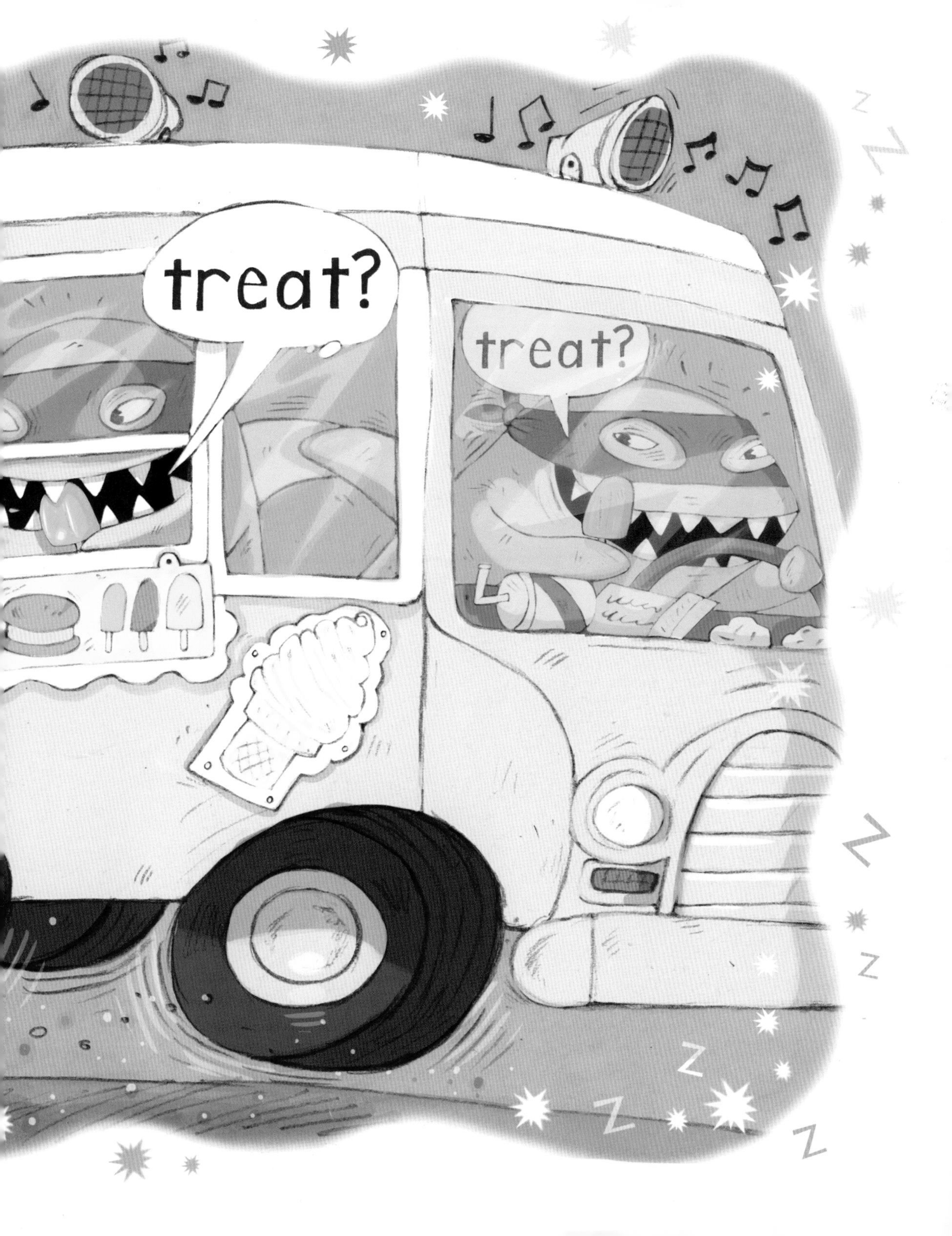
treat?
treat?

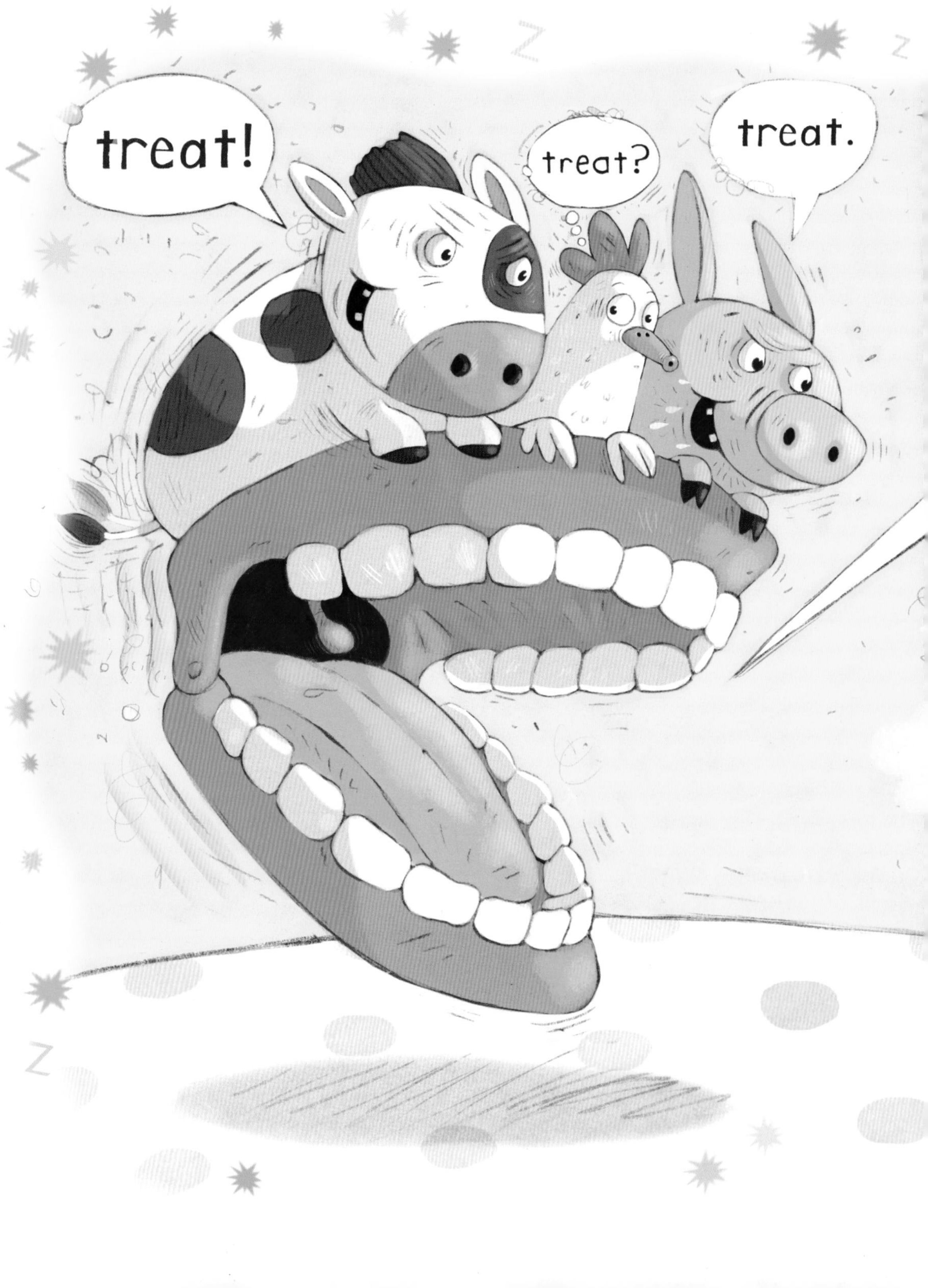
treat!
treat?
treat.

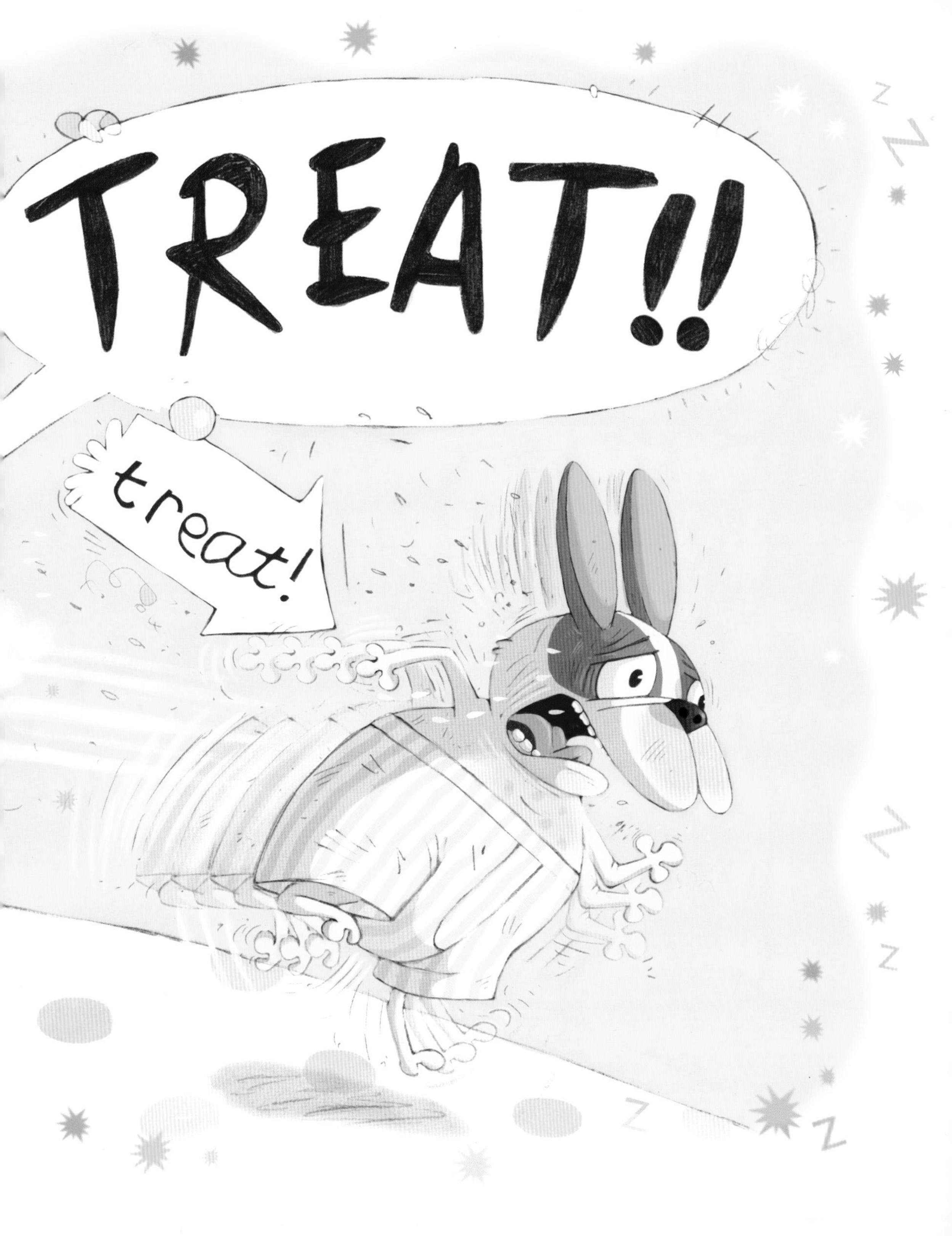
TREAT!!
treat!

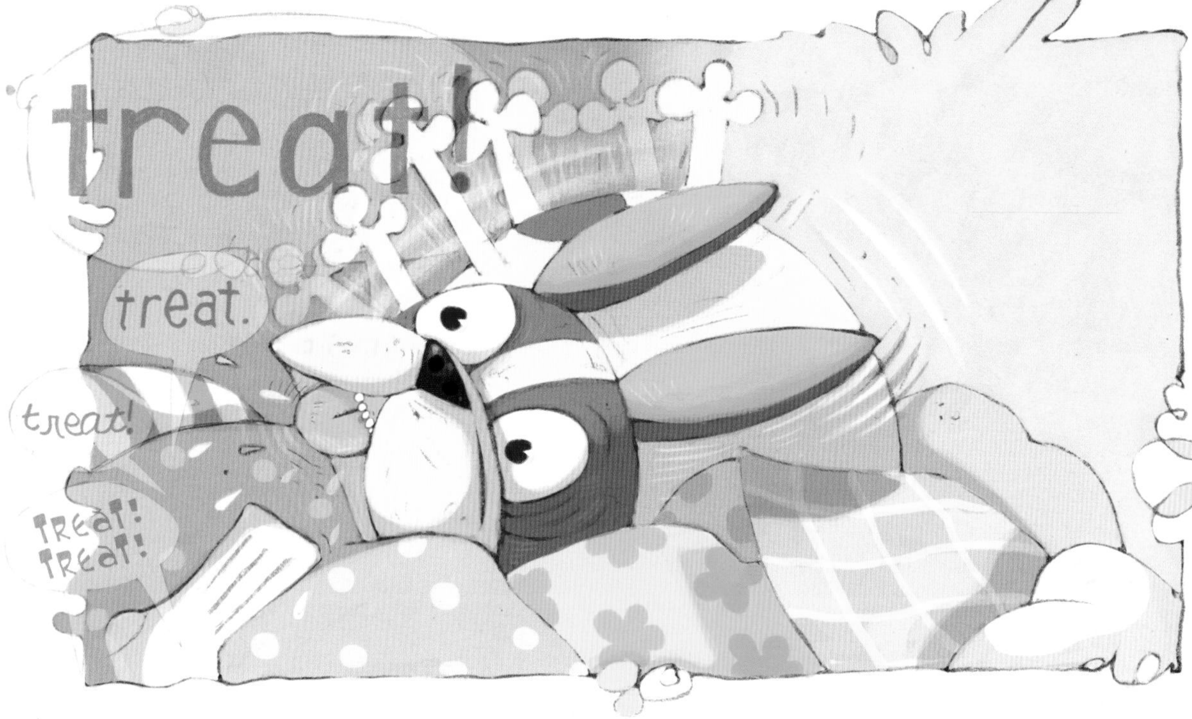
treat!
treat.
treat!
TREAT!
TREAT!

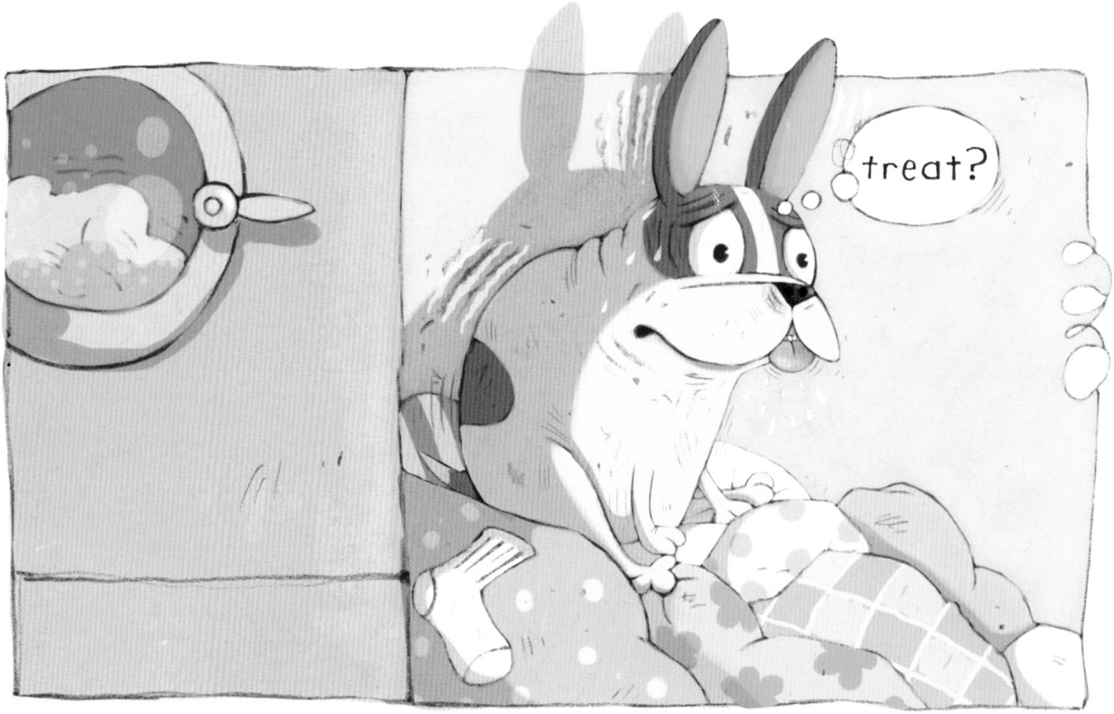
treat?

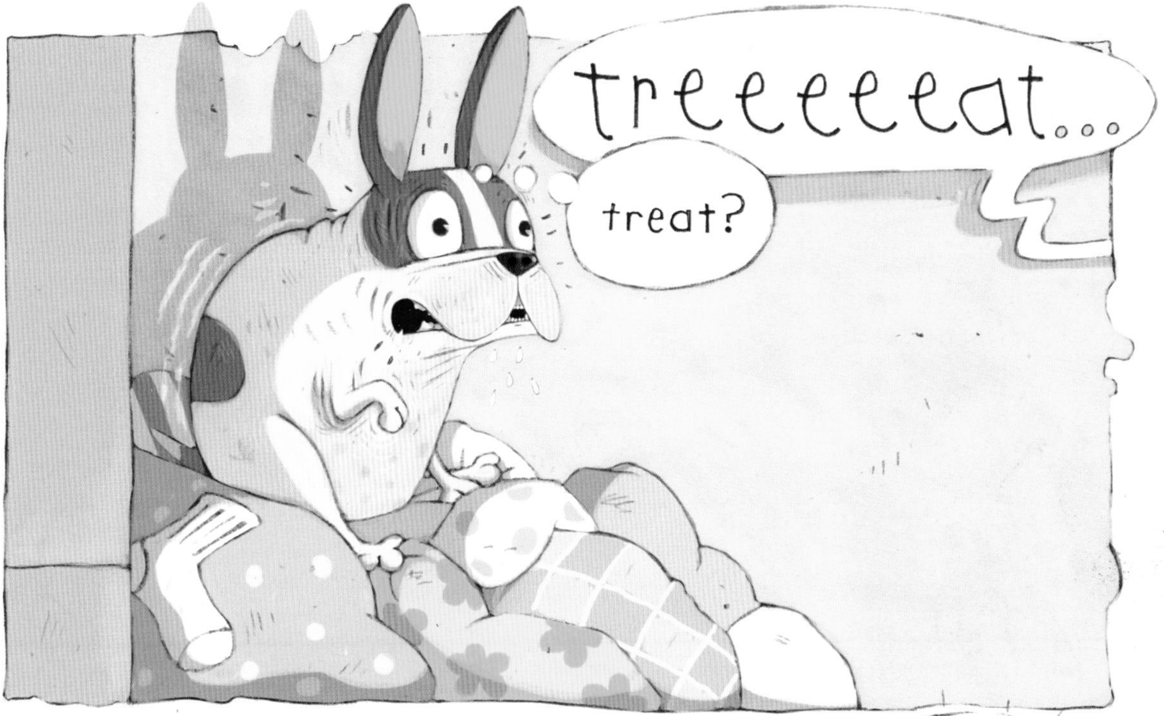
treeeeeat...
treat?

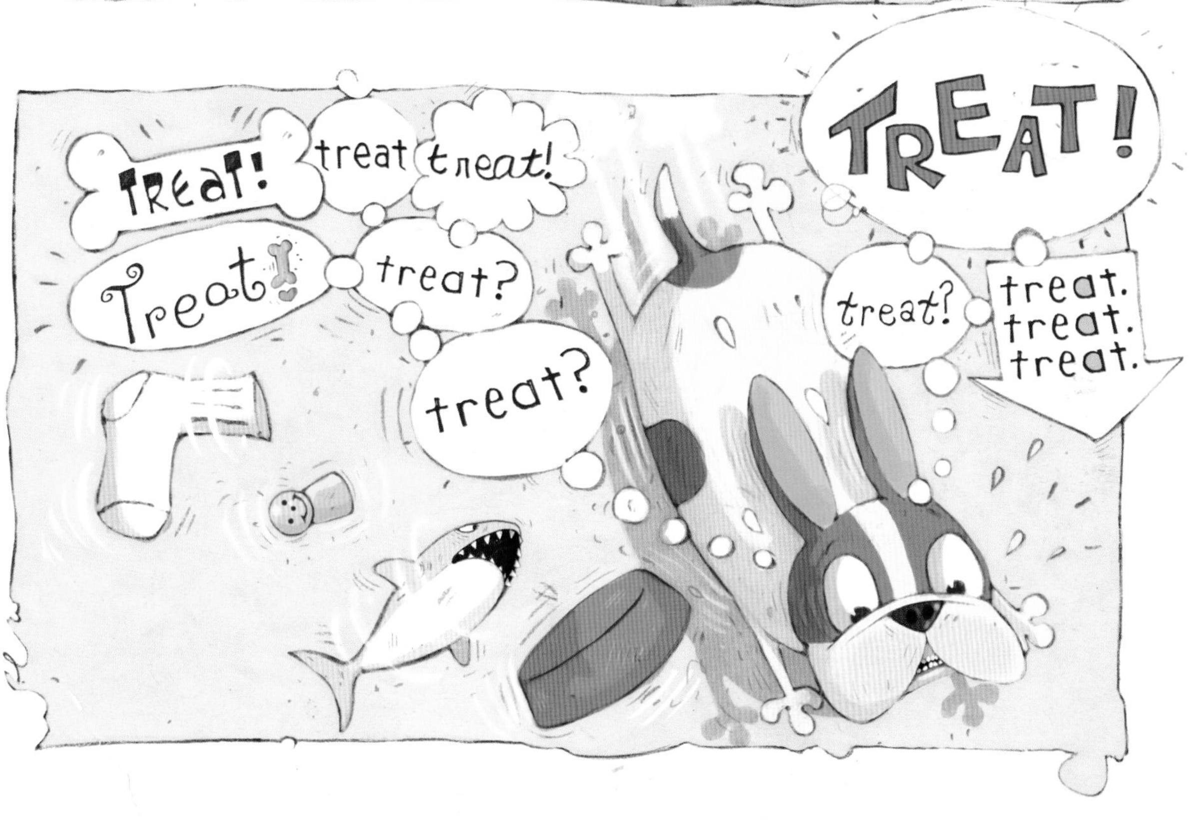
TREAT!
treat
treat!
Treat!
treat?
treat?
TREAT!
treat?
treat.
treat.
treat.

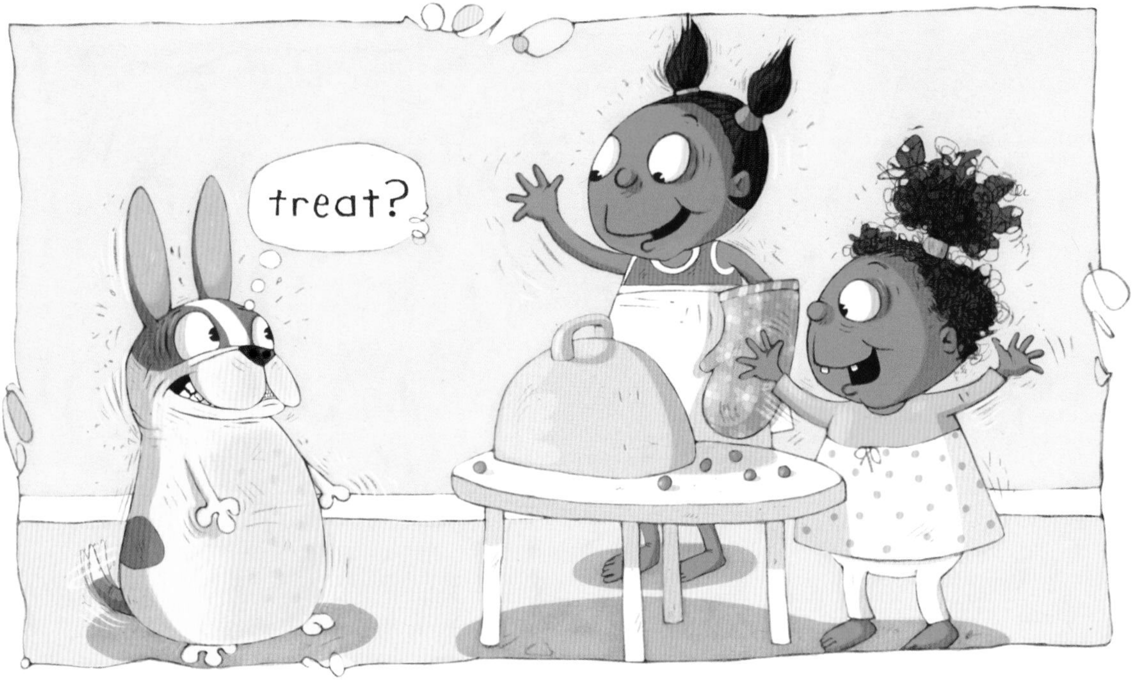
treat?

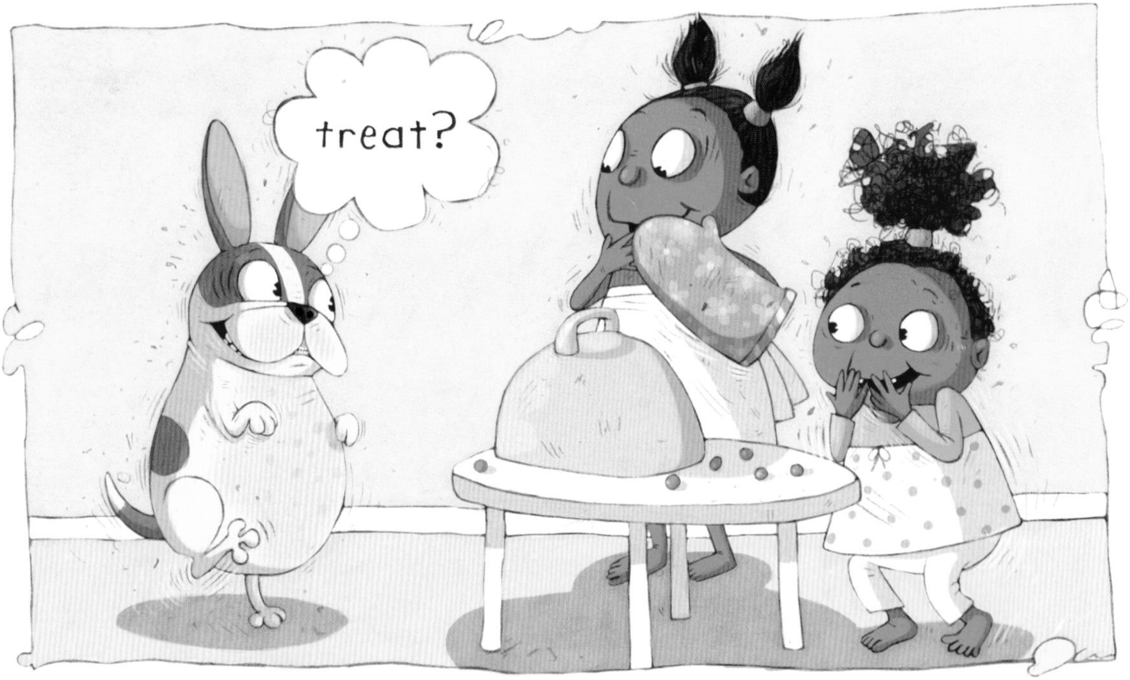
treat?

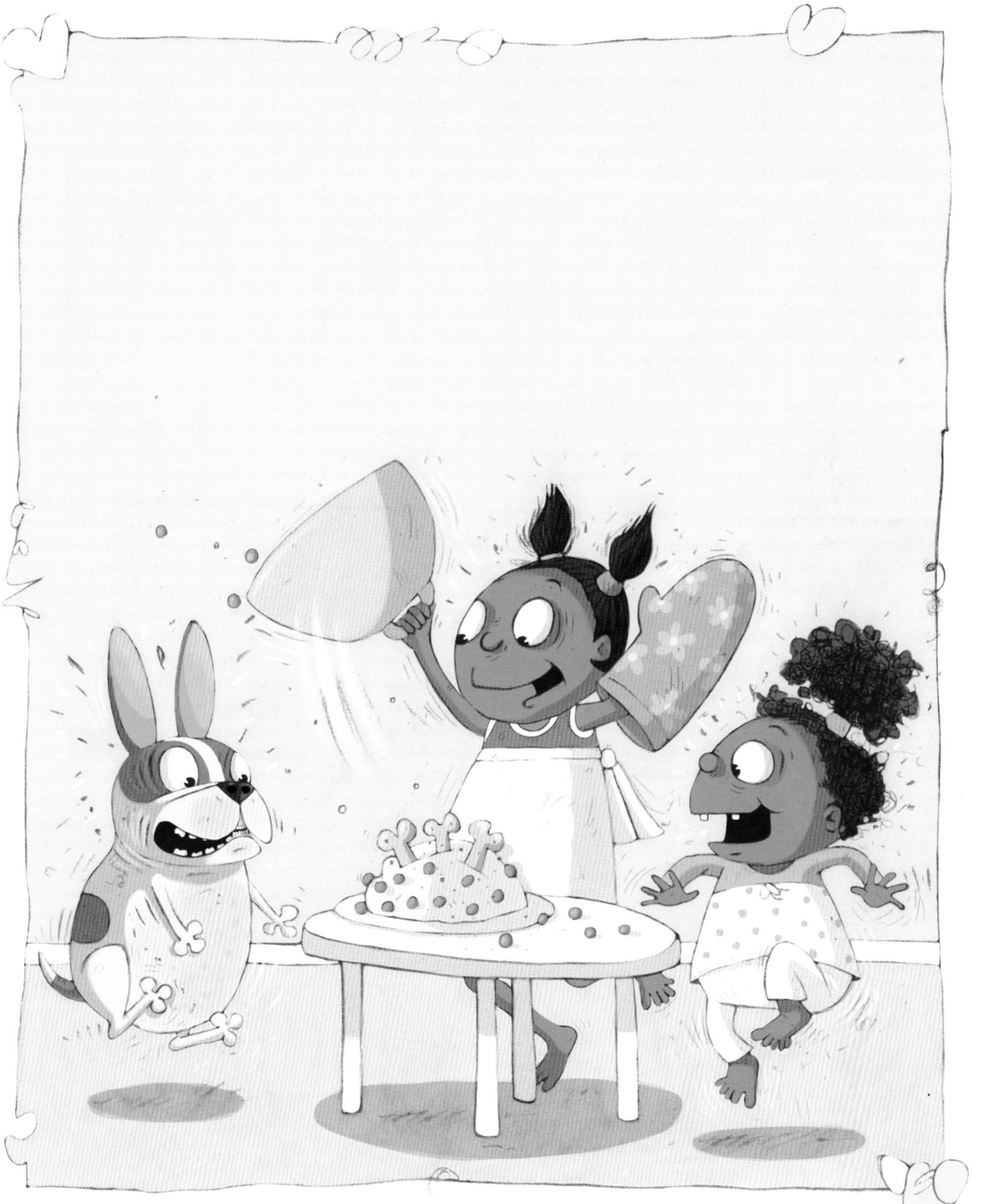

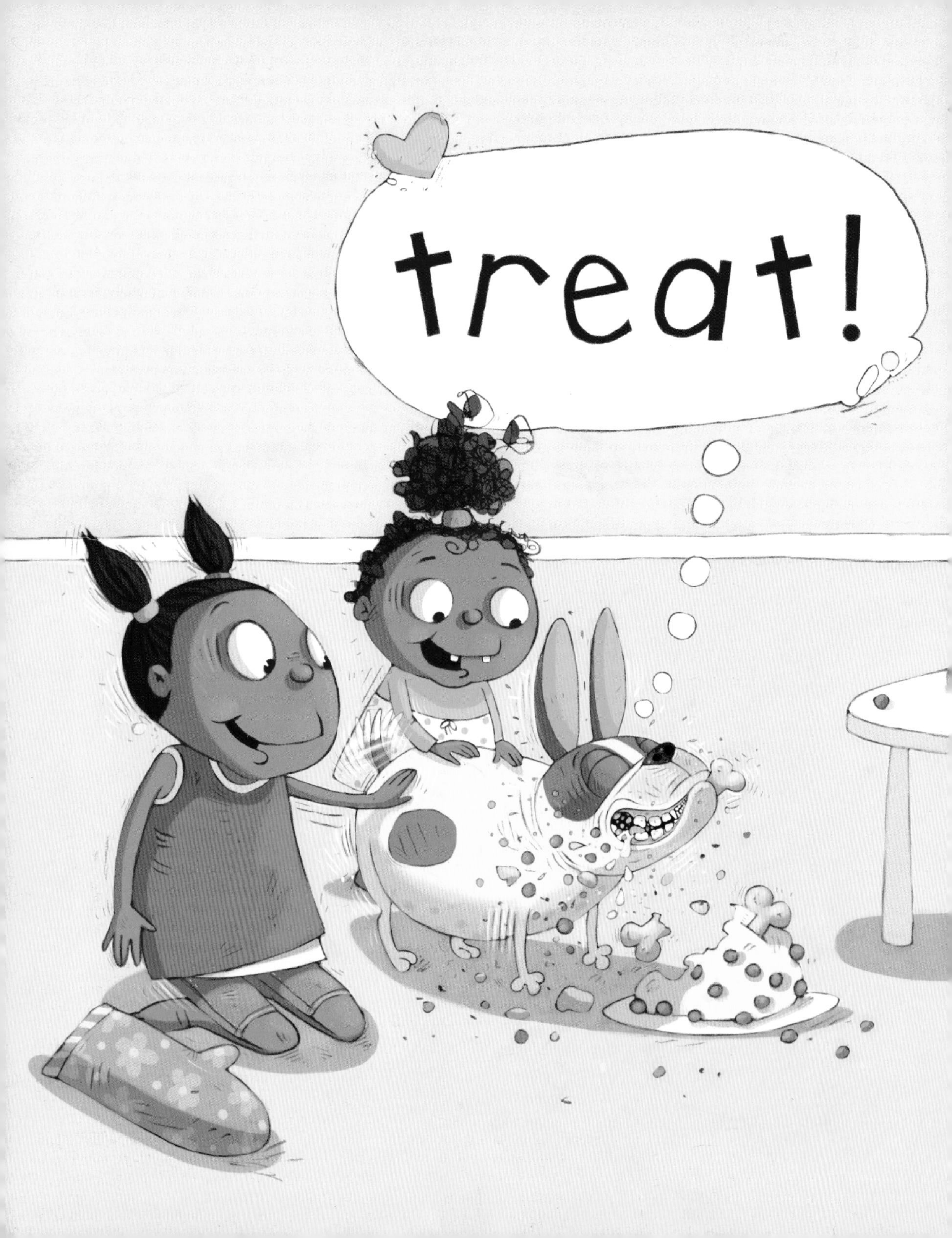
treat!

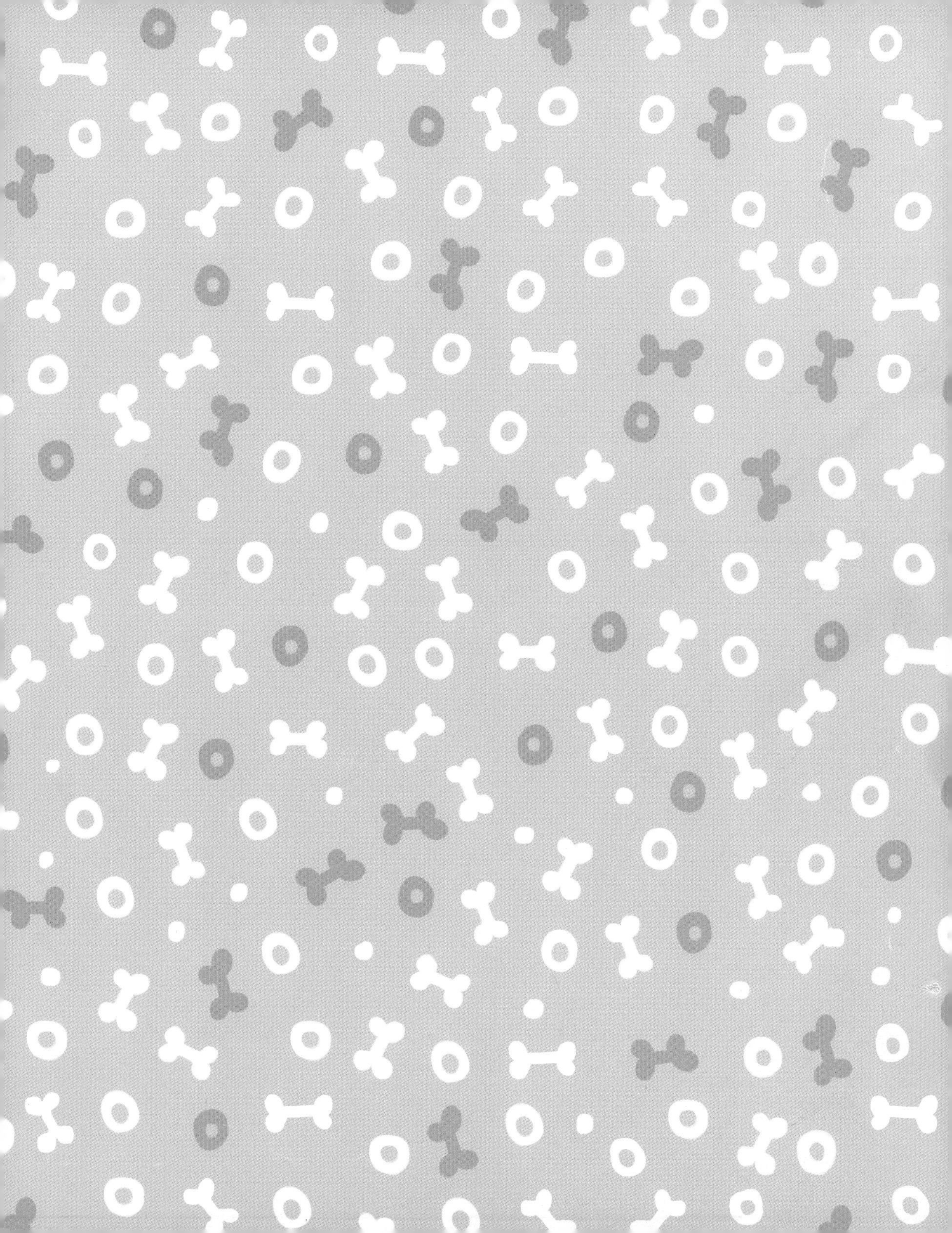